KU-523-322

POST MORTEM

Also by Peter Terrin in English translation
The Guard (2012)

Peter Terrin

POST MORTEM

Translated from the Dutch by
Laura Watkinson

MACLEHOSE PRESS
QUERCUS · LONDON

First published in the Dutch language as *Post Mortem*
by De Arbeiderspers, Amsterdam, in 2012
First published in Great Britain in 2015 by MacLehose Press
This paperback edition published in 2016 by

MacLehose Press
An imprint of Quercus Publishing Ltd
Carmelite House
50 Victoria Embankment
London EC4Y 0DZ

An Hachette UK company

Copyright © 2009 by Peter Terrin/De Arbeiderspers
English translation copyright © 2015 by Laura Watkinson

The translation of this book was funded by the
Flemish Literature Fund (www.flemishliterature.be)

Co-funded by the
Creative Europe Programme
of the European Union

Flemish
Literature
Fund

The moral right of Peter Terrin to be identified as
the author of this work has been asserted in accordance
with the Copyright, Designs and Patents Act, 1988.

Laura Watkinson asserts her moral moral right
to be identified as the translator of the work.

All rights reserved. No part of this publication may
be reproduced or transmitted in any form or by any means,
electronic or mechanical, including photocopy, recording,
or any information storage and retrieval system, without
permission in writing from the publisher.

A CIP catalogue record for this book is available
from the British Library.

ISBN (MMP) 978 1 78206 618 7
ISBN (Ebook) 978 1 78206 617 0

This book is a work of fiction. Names, characters,
businesses, organisations, places and events are either the
product of the author's imagination or are used fictitiously.
Any resemblance to actual persons, living or dead,
events or locales is entirely coincidental.

2 4 6 8 10 9 7 5 3 1

Designed and typeset in 11½/16pt Goudy by Patty Rennie
Printed and bound in Great Britain by Clays Ltd, St Ives plc

For my daughter

"We are not who we are,
we are what the world knows about us . . ."
                    W.F. Hermans,
              Memoirs of a Guardian Angel

She is born on 10 August, 2004: Renée Steegman. She leaves the womb at 14.56, a deep frown on her face. As I help Tereza to breathe, a midwife hovers over us, pushing against that huge belly. Tereza doesn't want to give birth, she wants to keep her child close, she knows how much she's going to miss her belly. She's ten days overdue, the gynaecologist says it needs to happen now. In the morning, we go to the hospital and they induce labour. I've brought a book with me, but read only half a page. Tereza is distressed, agitated, frightened. Then the pain comes, the epidural's too late. It looks like she's about to faint, right in the middle of giving birth – I don't know if that's possible, women fainting during labour, not with all that adrenalin in their blood. When the head appears, the gynaecologist says: Look, the head, she's got so much hair. But I don't want to see it, I don't want to look until she's really born, crying, living. I feel as if I still have everything to lose.

ONE

I

Like a blind man, he searched for the towel, arms outstretched. Opening his eyes would only make the stinging worse.

When was the last time he'd got shampoo in his eyes? He couldn't remember. Probably when he was a child. But maybe he often got shampoo in his eyes, better shampoo, shampoo that didn't sting. Or was he getting old, hypersensitive? Was he going to have to start using Renée's shampoo, the strawberry-scented one?

You're forty, thought Emiel Steegman. Forty's not old.

To make matters worse, not one single towel was hanging within reach on the chrome rack above the radiator.

He always tried, by setting a good example, by hanging the towels on the rack, to show others how they could please him with such a simple action. His attempts had failed.

His message had not been clear. They thought he was doing it to please them instead. And eventually they came to see it as normal.

How would Otto Richter deal with this situation? The famous, best-selling author obviously enjoyed the benefits of his advancing years these days, but what about when he was forty? Had he already had a younger, subservient wife to pay attention to such things as towels? What if the lack of a towel upset Richter so badly that his words abandoned him for the rest of the day? That was unthinkable. He employed a housekeeper. As with his sumptuous apartment in the capital's wealthiest neighbourhood, it didn't matter if he could afford a housekeeper or not. Writers were people who shaped the world to their own will, weren't they?

A flash of Tereza, his own wife, in a lace-trimmed pinafore, a cap on her head, and nothing else; she wasn't there about the towel.

He dismissed the thought, not enough time, but already he felt less appalled about her neglect.

He knocked over bottles, bath salts, toys, the big plastic frog with the small plastic frogs inside. Leaning on the edge of the bathtub, he reached out as far as he could for a towel that might be on the radiator. His eyes instinctively moved behind his closed eyelids, following his hands, looking at what he was imagining, and every movement intensified the stinging. Perhaps it was some neurological disorder, suddenly triggered by the heat of the gushing water. There is no remedy for this rare condition. Only painkillers can help, but they also make him feel groggy, so it's impossible to write. A few sentences a day, at most, typed with his eyes streaming. The rest of the time spent dozing on the sofa. Getting fat.

Why was he looking for a towel? How was a towel going to relieve the pain? Whatever was he thinking of?

He saw the map of Europe again, this time adorned with strange, moving stars, his eye muscles pushing them one way before they gradually slowed and shot off in another direction. When he was a child, in that initial darkness after the nightlight went out, the same kind of stars used to appear against the black interior of his eyes. Always two of them. At the time, they hadn't reminded him of stars, but of the glowing eyes of an owl, the rest of the bird invisible. It was a wise creature, watching over him; in his mind, never out loud, he called it Mr Owl. It stayed with him all night, disappearing just before he woke in the morning. He told no-one; it was as natural to him as having a father and a mother.

Perhaps his Mr Owl, which bore no resemblance to the Mr Owl in the children's T.V. show, had been an early sign of some latent ocular disorder.

He navigated the stars across the map of Europe, upwards, to the north-east, to the Baltic and the trio of former Soviet republics. He'd already briefed himself for the dinner, and knew, would never forget, that Estonia was the topmost of the three states, capital: Tallinn.

He'd also found a picture of one of the other guests on the internet. Presumably at the photographer's request, the author, a man of around his own age, had turned his least flattering side to the lens. Unless perhaps his other side was also afflicted by a lump of flesh in the crease of his nostril, which seemed unlikely. But it was even more unlikely that the Estonian author had deliberately allowed his ugly side to be photographed, as a statement to all those readers who think it important for books to be written by beautiful people, because in every other respect the man looked perfectly presentable, an amused smile on his lips, content with the world. In keeping with the intellectual image, he was wearing an open-necked shirt and a corduroy jacket. The photographer certainly had a sense of the aesthetic, but a clear vision was lacking.

The lump was not a classic wart, more like a growth, like a knot in a tree trunk, which would inevitably increase in size as the man grew older, making more and more of an impact on his face.

Perhaps, thought Steegman, as he heard the water dripping from his chin onto the tiled floor, he hadn't dared to challenge the photographer. An unknown writer, happy to have a promotional picture taken.

Because, of course, that was what they all were: unknown.

A dinner with good, unknown writers. Half of them from Estonia. Expertly organised by collaborating cultural bodies, who hoped to raise the profile of their country's literature. A select company – no more than twelve people, he'd been assured.

Charmed by their good intentions and by the undeniable honour of the invitation, he hadn't said no straight away.

He never said no straight away.

"No" could always come later. You never knew how something might be of benefit. From which direction that helping hand might come. Every little helps . . . Et cetera, et cetera. He detested the pettiness that well-meaning people kept trying surreptitiously to foist upon him.

Even after ten years of writing, after five books, he still had to content himself with small tokens of goodwill, such as midweek dinners with Estonian writers who were staying at a nearby castle for a month, and who were to be entertained in a suitably cultural fashion tomorrow evening. An exchange of intellectual capital. How many of his colleagues had declined the honour before the organisers, finally, had thought of him, of Steegman, always so grateful?

He let go of the edge of the bathtub and stood upright. Afraid of slipping, he slowly turned on his axis, and felt around for the tap. A towel was not going to solve anything.

It is written in the stars that he will end up sitting beside the man with the fleshy lump on his nose. For the duration of the entire meal, he'll be able to study the growth at close quarters. It robs him of any appetite and wakes him screaming in the middle of the night from his worst nightmare in years. The man, of course, is just as polite as he is himself. They top up each other's water, offer the bread basket. They enquire about each other's work with interest. He talks about his book that's about to come out, The Murderer, yes, that's right, it's his sixth, and together, the two of them solemnly raise a glass to the success of his new book, as if they've been friends for years. He doesn't burden the disfigured Estonian with his lack of confidence in the book's reception.

The showerhead sputtered and the heat came sliding down over his head like a long robe. The water sealed his ears. His voice, inside, was sonorous, serious: "Owing to a somewhat difficult situation at home." He waited for a moment and then repeated the words. "Owing to a some-what difficult situation at home."

He was particularly pleased with the word "somewhat".

When he'd repeated the sentence a third time, he knew that he'd formulated a viable excuse, largely because of that "somewhat". It was both vague and urgent. Mitigating, yet threatening. At first everything sounded fine, but still it was "somewhat difficult". The apology coming so late would make it all the more believable.

It also felt as if, with that one little word, he were confiding something personal to the organisation's managing director, without specifying what. His candour would be met with immediate understanding, as she would be reminded of her own concerns. In her reply to his email, within quarter of an hour, she would wish him all the best, promise discretion. If there was anything she could do . . .

He leaned with both hands against the wall, head bowed, as if starring in his own movie, a man confronted with "a difficult situation". He'd almost forgotten the stinging in his eyes, and now he turned his face into the hard jets of water, but did not dare to look.

He saw the managing director, the tulips in the elegant vase on the linen tablecloth. She's waiting for her husband, who has cooked for her – he's gone to get the pepper. She could mention it now, across the cooking island, but she waits, appreciatively inhaling the spicy vapours rising from her plate. She's a woman of nearly fifty, goes to the hairdresser's every week. You'll never guess what happened, she says to Hans or Henk, as he smiles and pulls up a chair. Steegman, you know the one, blond hair, those glasses with the chunky frame? He's cancelled. He's not coming to the dinner. Dropped me a line today. It must be something serious. Something to do with his wife or his daughter. Steegman never says no.

He decided to do a countdown, as he would with Renée. It was the only way. But when he reached two, to prove to himself that he was a man, he opened his eyes. He had to force them to stay open, resist the reflex to shut them. He thought he could feel every one of those sharp jets of water making a tiny dent in his soft eyeballs. Again he decided to count, up to ten this time, and by then the rest of the foam should have washed away. But he counted to twenty because, by the time he'd got to five, staring into the splashing mist was beginning to feel pleasant. By twenty, the stinging had turned into a new, unfamiliar sensation, which seemed a lot like dehydration.

After some blinking and rubbing, he looked around, as a test. Everything in the bathroom was in its usual place. The aquamarine wall tiles from the late 1950s, at shoulder height all around the room, still dominated the space, conjuring up images of beautiful swimming pools in summertime. The bidet with the broken tap. The dusty pots and bottles on the wooden shelves, with the towels below. The large washstand, the mirror, flecked with brown, the brightly coloured fish with their swirling tail fins, swimming in a line across the window.

He couldn't feel the stinging anymore. His vision was sharp, without glasses. More clearly than ever, he could see the objects that had worked their way into this house and worn themselves into his life.

Steegman stacked the post he'd collected over the past four days into a neat pile on the corner of the dining table. On the top was an envelope from a bank. Lodewijk. The first name of his neighbour from across the road stood out, there in the address window, the image of the word. Lodewijk. You so rarely saw that name anywhere these days, only in announcements of births or deaths.

They'd met two years ago, on Lodewijk's front lawn, soon after moving in. Lodewijk gave Steegman permission to call him "Wiet" or "Wietje", which is what everyone else in the street and the village called him. Steegman decided, when no explanation was forthcoming, that it must be derived from "Louis", the French equivalent of Lodewijk. But something about Lodewijk's posture, something about his shoulders, something around the corners of his mouth indicated that he was not really the kind of man who went for diminutives and nicknames, and that he used that name, or had permitted it to be used, just to create a certain impression. To curry favour with the villagers, to show he was one of them, to be accepted. But that, deep down, in the seclusion of his own living room, at night, he felt an aversion, bordering on loathing, to anyone who dared to call him "Wietje". He was a retired bank clerk with forty-four years of loyal service! The riff-raff! How dare they?

At the same time Steegman knew his neighbour would take offence if he didn't accept the invitation. It would be tantamount to rejecting the man himself. As if Steegman, the city slicker, refused to accept that Lodewijk was just a humble, amiable villager. He'd be seen as arrogant.

The conversation lasted nearly ten minutes. He kept on practising in his mind, so he'd remember to say "Wiet" at least once. In the end, though, he couldn't bring himself to utter that ridiculous name. He felt no inclination to address a man he barely knew as "Wiet". The man's insistence felt like a violation of his privacy. So when he left, he just gave him a friendly smile and went for "Lodewijk". It was, after all, the man's name.

He saw no reaction on Lodewijk's face. Perhaps he thought Steegman wanted first to earn the familiarity he'd so generously offered. Or worse, that he meant to start using the name when they next met. But, to Steegman, those three carefully enunciated syllables had sounded like hammer-blows on a flagpole marking out his territory.

The pile of post in one hand, Renée holding the other, he headed down the path from the front door, at the side of the house, to the street.

He was thinking about the blue basket.

The day after they came back from holiday last year, Lodewijk, as early as the usual postman, had come round with his blue basket. The post, which he'd taken from the letterbox at Steegman's request, had been stacked in the

13

basket and separated by sheets of A4 paper with the day and the date noted on them in calligraphic handwriting. In date order, with important correspondence on top of junk mail.

Steegman had thanked him profusely.

Lodewijk didn't want the basket back straight away. He looked at it and said he didn't need it right now, that they could take their time to go through everything. When there was no reaction to this statement, he added that the next day would be fine. Sometime in the morning. As it happened, he and his wife would be out tomorrow afternoon. But Steegman could return the basket in the morning. He asked if that was convenient, and when Steegman nodded he said, "Good. Then it's agreed. Tomorrow, before midday." Tereza's attempts simply to take the post out of the basket and put it on the table were met with violent protestation. Lodewijk really didn't need the basket for anything. And the next day would be fine. Before twelve thirty. Because his wife wanted to leave by half twelve at the latest, Lodewijk said, looking Steegman in the eyes.

It really wasn't much of a basket. Ancient, baby-blue plastic from the 1960s. Steegman couldn't imagine what other use Lodewijk might have for it.

He hadn't needed a basket for Lodewijk's post. Their holiday was only five days, hiking in Alsace. The post would easily have fitted into Renée's little hand.

At the end of the street, two sharp explosions in an exhaust pipe – a small car shot forward. A body-kit hid the wheels, the front spoiler hanging so close to the road that it could have cleared snow. Inside the car, a massive drum thudded away. Steegman could feel Renée's fear, the way she hesitated to take that step onto the pavement.

This was what made their quiet street, no more than one hundred and fifty metres in length, so dangerous. Unhindered by other road users, tempted by the slope, drivers went hurtling downhill. At first, Steegman had wanted to run after the reckless morons and teach them a lesson, like Garp in the film adaptation of the book. But Garp was a wrestler. Steegman couldn't remember now if he actually used physical violence. But every idiot who raced through this residential area filled him with visions of frenzied violence. He dragged them out of the car, ordered them to stand up straight while he thumped them in the face a few times with his bare fist. He offered no explanation to the wailing boy racers. When they were lying on the ground, bleeding, barely conscious, he turned his back on them and went home. No witnesses dared to speak to him or try to stop him. Most of them nodded their approval.

But Steegman had never hit anyone in the face. He'd always avoided conflict, his sense of self-preservation getting the better of his fury. So he just gave the speed demons his filthiest look from a distance. Standing there on the pavement, it was the best he could come up with. Making gestures would only provoke aggression. He gave them the dirtiest look that a university-educated father with a comfortable career could summon up. At best, his furious gaze bounced off the windscreen like a pebble, making the driver blink. But usually it was more like a blossom petal or a dandelion seed, caught on the breeze, skirting the entire length of the car without ever touching it.

All that could be seen sticking up above the steering wheel was the long peak of a cap. The driver stared out like a toddler peeking over the edge of a bathtub, jolted around by every little irregularity in the road surface.

As this pandemonium roared past them, Steegman instinctively squeezed Renée's hand. Thirty metres down the road, the little car had to brake hard to avoid being launched into space by the raised crossing. The exhaust boomed again, a flame shooting out of the pipe.

"That car's on fire."

"No, sweetheart. It just looks like it. Look, it's already stopped."

"Why has it stopped?"

"Yes, it's a shame, isn't it?"

"Why?"

He cast a glance at the nearby houses to see if any windows were open. But there was still enough noise, from the engine, from the drum, to drown out his words. What exactly did he think anyone was going to catch him doing, anyway?

"If the car was still burning, the red fire engine would have to come and put out the flames."

Irritation at the silly tone of voice he was using to speak to her. It was false jollity, it was patronising, the way you were supposed to speak to children, intended for the ears of anyone who might be listening.

"Why?"

That vacant, automatic "why" – any attempts to answer it were futile, as they would all be met with the same "why".

"First we look left," he said. "Then we look right, and then left again."

Renée looked straight ahead. On the other side of the street, a three-legged cat hopped onto the road. Its stump was neatly covered with fur, as if the animal had been born that way. Suddenly, an ominous image of a half-dead pedigree cat that he'd forgotten to put food out for. Its pale-grey fur still thick and gleaming, the eyes a little surprised. Charlie, the couple's beloved pet for eleven years now, languishing in their rattan chair. But he was almost certain Lodewijk hadn't mentioned any pets. No, Lodewijk and pets – that didn't fit.

It was nine thirty and the sun was shining on the fronts of the houses across the road. He'd once described it in a novel – although he couldn't instantly bring to mind which one – the effect that this kind of sun, in both spring and autumn, has on the objects it touches. How the intensity, the saturation of colours, makes it seem as if the houses are not dead matter, not bricks and mortar, but living creatures, waiting patiently, silently, along countless roads for their moment to come.

They knew that he knew.

These houses were detached, they were simple but solid homes from a time when the absence of any particular architectural style was the fashion – unlike his house, distinctly conventional. A mishmash, "charming" the most they could aspire to. Most of them were still occupied by the original owners.

The shutters of Lodewijk's house had been lowered to ten centimetres above the window ledge. Whenever it rained, the shutters were closed, too. What went on inside that house when it was raining had long been a mystery to him. Until he realised that a shutter would protect the glass from splashes, so it would gleam for longer, and need less cleaning.

The cat hopped across the road without slowing down.

Steegman and Renée did not exist, its ears faced firmly forward. The street was a surface that had been smoothed over for the cat's convenience, to aid its passage from one garden to another.

Steegman snorted.

Jealous of a three-legged cat.

Lodewijk accepted the little stack of post as if it were a gift. He was delighted. The post must have been the last in a long list of worries associated with a five-day holiday. Now the trip really was over. With his post in his hands, he was finally safe at home.

Lodewijk's wife wholeheartedly recommended hiking in Alsace. Especially in the springtime. She told him she had the same feeling every year, as if she could taste the oxygen in the air on her tongue. One of her friends had it too, but Lodewijk didn't get it at all. They'd been going there for thirty-two years now, five days in Alsace, with the same group of friends, married couples. Thirty-two years!

Then she paused and gave him a strange look out of the corner of her eye, somehow overfamiliar. She was a refined kind of woman, tastefully dressed, with a lady-like name that he found hard to remember. He stuck to "Mrs" instead, just as he continued to use "Lodewijk", as did she. As a result, she saw him as a man of culture, an ally; he should understand the look she was giving him better than anyone. Was she asking his forgiveness for this absurd display of middle-class persistence? Or was she playing up her embarrassment to obtain his approval, to elicit his understanding for her pride, which of course had no foundation. Perhaps she was saying: look, this is life, here, now. Escaping from it is an illusion as big as Alsace.

As she focused her attention on Renée, asking how old she was and enthusiastically counting the three tiny fingers she held up, Lodewijk leafed through his post without opening anything. A pleasure for later, when he was alone.

Had the managing director already opened the message in her inbox? Steegman had sent his email about an hour before, referring to "a somewhat difficult situation at home". Or was it stuck on a server somewhere, in digital limbo, forever out of reach? "A somewhat difficult situation at home." What would the managing director, perched on the edge of a colleague's desk, holding a cup of coffee in front of her face, read into his cryptic formulation?

What would it have made him imagine?

Relationship issues, first of all, or a serious illness. A very serious illness, fatal, discovered only recently during a routine examination. Bad news, certainly, even though absolutely nothing was wrong. Not a cloud in the sky.

A sense of playing with fire. A sense of wishing something upon oneself, misfortune, upon one's family, by resorting to such measures. Was there some line that you crossed at risk to your own life, a moral boundary? Or had that mitigating "somewhat" given him a valid passport?

Lodewijk asked how they were settling in. How long they'd been living in the village now.

"Two years. In June."

"Two years? Is it already two years? How about that? Doesn't time fly? Must be quite a difference from the city, eh, our little village?"

Steegman explained that they'd made their decision mainly because of the surrounding hills, because of the peace and quiet, because he himself had grown up in the countryside, in the polders. Diplomatically, he confessed that they'd based their decision on both the area and the house, the house and the garden in particular, not to mention the price, and not so much on the charms of this particular village, which were limited to the market square and its plane trees.

"Yes, the house is quite something. Semi-detached. A family of bakers. Didn't skimp on it either. Plenty of money. A bakery, doing good business. Must have been a real gold mine back then."

Lodewijk had put the post on the desk and was leaning with both hands on the high back of one of the dining chairs.

"Almost three generations. Did you know that, two years ago, the house still belonged to a well-known baking family? The left, your side, is where the brother lived, with the sister and their mother on the right. And the poorly little mite, of course . . ."

"No," said Steegman.

"No," said Lodewijk. "No, I thought not." He looked through the French windows into the back garden. "That estate agent didn't know either. Some young whippersnapper in a skinny tie, you could have knocked him down with a feather when he heard. But his boss must have known."

"Ah," his wife chipped in cheerily. "It's all such a long time ago, no-one's bothered about all that now. What do you think, sweetheart? Would you like a glass of milk? Or something else? Apple juice? I'm sure big girls who are three years old like apple juice, don't they?"

The back garden was bustling, but meticulously maintained. Shrubs, flowers and plants. Terracotta and pergola, no corner unused. The many-sided lawn had been mown in concentric circles. The grass gleamed.

"No, thank you. We have to get home to Mummy. Next time, eh, Renée?"

Lodewijk's wife still had Renée's hand clasped between hers. The little girl didn't dare to pull away. The words "apple juice" hadn't even registered with her.

"What's that I saw?" asked Lodewijk suddenly. "In your garden? What do you have in your garden?"

"My swing," said Renée, with a little skip in her voice.

"A swing, just for you?"

"And a slide."

"Oh, you're such a lucky little girl. Do you know that? Do you like playing in the garden?"

"Yes."

"A big garden's nice. But it's a lot of work for Daddy. Fun for the kiddywinks, lots of work for Daddy."

Since they'd moved in, all Steegman had done was mow the lawn. He didn't think much more needed doing. A garden like a park. Was Lodewijk's remark meant as a slap on the wrist or a pat on the back? Before he could come up with a reply, Lodewijk walked over to the desk and opened a drawer.

"Do you collect these cards? Smurfs. There's a Smurf on every card. They're for you, because your daddy collected our post."

He bent down deeply beside Renée and fanned out the cards. "Look, you see this one here? Which Smurf is that?"

"Brainy Smurf."

"No. It's Writer Smurf! Like your daddy!" He winked without looking at him, clownish, half of his face and mouth alarmingly contorted. "They're fun, these cards. The supermarket's giving them away free with your shopping."

"First left, then right. And then left again."

The street was silent.

The rhododendron by the bay window was probably dead. The rosebush beside the path was a tangled mess. The roof was high, but still the birch tree towered above it, overshadowing the shed at the bottom of the garden.

A family of bakers.

The exterior walls were made of small yellow glazed bricks; they had not yet lost their subtle sheen. As the front doors were at the sides, it wasn't immediately obvious from the street that it was in fact two houses. It looked like one spacious building with a large first floor extending over a half-sunken double garage.

A house for a managing director.

Only the net curtains, on the left, and the faded FOR SALE board, on the right, suggested otherwise.

"A somewhat difficult situation at home."

The sentence can no longer be deleted.

If his work should ever come to the attention of a large readership, if ever, against his express wishes, a biographer should delve into his life after his death and pore through his email to come across this mysterious little phrase, he'll be convinced that he's found a clue. He'll think he's onto something, something of great importance, which the author didn't want to reveal, which he alluded to only in this phrase: an incident that deserves at least a chapter in his book, maybe more, maybe even the central point of the biography, around which the other stories can orbit like satellites: *the* defining event in the life and work of Emiel Steegman. He will hunt it down like a man possessed.

But there was nothing wrong. Nothing at all.

23

3

A blood-ripe cherry, the darkest one in the small bag that his mum has given him. Eight cherries. It's not much, and yet it's an abundance. Something to look forward to, something good to come. Eight little events.

He pops the cherry between his lips, cushions it like a pearl in the hollow of his tongue. Swings his leg over the saddle and pushes off.

The housing estate is empty. The houses are turned in upon themselves. Only the occasional car, or a tilted garage door, betrays the presence of people. Those who see him have no idea. They think: the boy from number 9, out on his bike. A blond boy of thirteen, they think. A blue bike. Some see the freezer bag dangling from the right-hand handlebar, but it doesn't sink in. Emiel, though, they do see him – that's for sure. If there's some crime, an investigation, someone will testify: the boy from number 9, just after midday. But the blood-ripe cherry in his mouth? No, they don't have a clue about that, not there, inside their red, uniform houses, not those people.

He barely sucks on it. The firm flesh is still intact within the tight, smooth skin. Now and then he swallows his saliva, which has no flavour. The street where he lives is on a slope, his feet follow the slow rotation of the pedals, feel the gear biting into the chain.

In front of Andy's house, two streets away, he does a couple of circuits. Andy's bike is lying on the grass. The thick net curtain behind the large window falls in perfect folds. They no longer bother calling for each other these days.

Above the beet field, the air shimmers. The leaves hang limply from the fat heads sticking up from the earth. The sheep shed beyond the field flickers like a flame. He props his bike with one pedal against the high kerbstone of the road, which is still under construction. He sits down, beside the front wheel, pushes the cherry into his cheek, applies pressure, but the fruit holds firm. He has a close-up view of the ants in the dry, sandy gutter, the white hair growing on his shins.

He keeps an eye on the bend, where the new part of the estate joins the old. All the traffic will eventually travel along this road, all the bricks for all the houses. The map has already been laid out in kerbstones, among Farmer Tuyt's meadows and his fields of maize and beet.

His cheek and gums have grown used to the cherry that separates them. It's become a part of his mouth, and removal is not a pain-free process; grimacing, he polishes the cherry on the hem of his T-shirt. Then he holds it between thumb and forefinger like a tiny, brightly gleaming apple and tentatively takes a minuscule bite. As his incisors break through the resistance, his mouth lights up and, with it, the street, the housing estate and the holidays.

4

The photographer was driving an old Volvo. A considered, style-conscious choice, without a doubt; he's one of the best-known portrait photographers in the country. With no more than a shoulder bag, he walked up the garden path, his steps slow and irregular, a man deliberating with himself. When the bell rang, Steegman still jumped. For a few seconds, he stood motionless on the rug in the front room. He saw the fragmented figure in the frosted glass of the wrought-iron screen door, heard him clear his throat. As soon as his heel clicked on the tiled floor, Steegman could no longer go back.

The publisher strongly advised placing a portrait of the author on the back cover. Readers wanted a face to go with the name. Without a photograph, he might as well be dead.

He had difficulties with his own image, the confrontation was an ordeal. The issue wasn't his appearance, this wasn't about handsome or ugly. He wasn't handsome, he knew that, but he didn't think he was ugly, or at least he couldn't imagine Tereza going for an ugly man, not the kind of "ugly" that everyone swiftly agrees on – no, she was too attractive for that. And he couldn't imagine falling for a woman for whom his physical appearance was of absolutely no significance: a woman like that, no matter how beautiful, wouldn't be capable of exciting him. He recognised how vain such thoughts were, and was also aware that vanity was definitely not the sole preserve of beautiful people. Perhaps Tereza had fallen for the vanity that her love had triggered, which had the capacity to transform an average man into an alluring lover. Maybe, probably, that meant he was interchangeable. But as long as she didn't exchange him, he didn't think he was ugly.

The common lament of people who said they didn't recognise themselves in a photograph or a video, who felt their self-image didn't coincide with their actual image, was alien to him. He always recognised himself. He knew who he was, he could see it in his eyes, in his hair and ears, his high forehead, a combination with little to no character, banal. He would have preferred not to recognise himself. He didn't want a photograph that merely reinforced what was already there in print. A photograph should bring something to light, reveal something, provide him with something that undermined his convictions, proof that he was wrong.

They drank espresso in the front room, the photographer slurping as he sipped, recalling a trip to Mexico, a journey through the jungle, twenty-three days without coffee. He was a handsome man with jet-black hair and deep-set eyes that regarded him warmly. He asked about the house. It surprised him, this, here, in the countryside. It was a compliment, of course, and yet it saddled Steegman with the awkward feeling that he had to explain himself. He was, of course, an unknown; it would be impossible for him to afford this house with the royalties from his books. The suspicion that he was living off his wife or prematurely squandering his parents' inheritance was something he liked to get out of the way as quickly as possible. A bargain, all agreed in a single day. "A family of bakers," the photographer repeated, taking another good look around, as if searching for traces of them.

Steegman leaned against the window frame, turned his face towards the cloudy afternoon. The photographer swore by natural light. He used an old Leica and rolls of Kodak film with just twelve large negatives. He had never worked in colour. His photographs could be recognised from a distance. Stark, composed images that mercilessly accentuated the earthly, the transitory, which ultimately made them appear romantic.

Steegman had worn a white shirt and a skinny black tie for the occasion. The photographer asked him about his choice, and Steegman told him about his nostalgia for the years of classic typewriters and filterless cigarettes, femmes fatales and tailor-made suits, detectives and existential novels. He showed him the glossy black Underwood Champion from 1937, Alfred Hitchcock's favourite model. When the photographer placed his Leica beside the typewriter to type a few words, it was like a family reunion.

An inhuman length of time passed before the photographer pressed the button.

He took every attempt seriously, waiting for the right image to appear, as if it were his last chance. Often he didn't even press the button, but glanced, without speaking, over his Leica at Steegman, before ducking back down. His directions were minimal. Steegman felt as if he were being examined; he held his breath, felt his heart thumping in his throat, didn't know what to do with his mouth, which kept cramping up.

He thought about his Estonian colleague with the lump on his nose, a man he might never meet. And about how, as unknown authors, the success of both of them, a success to which they would never raise a glass at a dinner in a castle, could depend in part on their photographs. That first introduction to potential readers. How long will they pause to look at their pictures? Will they like the Estonian for not hiding his flaws? Will they consider the possibility that this actually is his best side, that the other side is in an even worse state? That he is, in fact, just as vain as a man in a crisp white shirt with a skinny black tie? Will someone, somewhere, in a bookshop, surrounded by thousands of other books, thousands of blurbs and just as many photographs, understand Steegman's tongue-in-cheek reference?

It was more likely that not one conscious thought would occur during that brief encounter. That it was enough, was a success, if some aspect of the picture caught some-one's attention. Tie or fleshy lump, fur collar or turned-up nose, it didn't matter what, as long as it was something.

Steegman could see his reflection in the lens. He asked the photographer if he should look deep into the Leica, at the shutter, or focus his gaze on his reflection in front. If the eyes are the mirror of the soul, he laughed, he'd rather not be squinting on his book cover.

*

Early that evening, he received an email from the managing director. He was in his office, a small room upstairs at the front of the house. He was sitting in the chair covered with the fleece of the sheep his parents had once shared with their neighbours, and upon which he'd written all of his books. He looked at the words on the screen and heard Lodewijk mowing the grass in his front garden. And in his typical, illogical way, he incorporated the managing director's email and Lodewijk's lawnmower into his dream, a dream that seemed to last all night: one big, obvious puzzle that didn't require a solution, that was just a feeling. The managing director in a terracotta-coloured suit, telling him to forget about the dinner and to concentrate on the important things in his life, and then Lodewijk turning his mower upside down and pointing at the different blades, so many more than an ordinary mower, and they shred the mown grass instantly, so there's no need to clear it up and it becomes natural fertiliser for the lawn. Grass as compost for grass. Then the managing director and Lodewijk studiously turn their backs on his house, while he goes on watching and sees someone opening the net curtain in his office, not Tereza, not Renée, a stranger with his own physique, with similar glasses, but with dark hair, who waves at him and says something he can't hear through the window, talking as if Steegman were standing beside him in the office, a long story.

As he stepped into the shower the next day, without having spoken to Tereza or Renée, even to say good morning, as he closed his eyes again and submitted to the rushing water, he recognised that very rare feeling, he knew something was on its way, that he didn't have to do anything else now, just breathe and stay alive, transport oxygen to his brain, and wait. He suppressed any hint of excitement, concentrated on the sound of the water, stood still. And here, in the place where the day before he'd got shampoo in his eyes and concocted that phrase for the managing director, was where it happened, as if a spin dryer were whizzing around at the same speed as the blades in Lodewijk's lawnmower, and inside its drum was everything that had happened in the previous twenty-four hours, everything that inspired him; he had to trust in his legs to keep him upright, and then suddenly a single drop of the extract fell, fresh as menthol, potent as Jean-Baptiste Grenouille's ultimate, virginal perfume, into the space behind his forehead, changing everything: an idea. An idea for a new novel.

A quarter of an hour later, he stirred himself, reaching for the towel, which was hanging from the chrome rack where it should be.

5

At first glance, breakfast today was no different from yesterday. Outside, through the large windows, the fresh blueness; inside, the white tablecloth, the tapping of spoons on china and Honeypops enthusiastically being crushed in Renée's half-open mouth, on the other side of the table. But inside Steegman's head, nothing was as it had ever been before. That space was now occupied by his plan to write a novel about a writer.

He wasn't that kind of writer, but he thought it should be allowed, just this once; after all, writers were people, too.

Out of the corner of his eye, he looked at Tereza. He'd always given her the exclusive in the past; he didn't dare to talk to anyone else about a new book for the first time. It was too soon, he realised, far too soon. The idea was sketchy and abstract, it needed a few scenes to flesh it out first, so that an outsider would find something familiar in it. It would hit her like a dead weight. There'd be none of that instant enthusiasm, and Tereza, lovingly, would try to work it all out by asking him questions he could not answer. Questions that would raise doubts, relevant questions, capable of quietly demolishing this bare framework.

A name. He had to come up with a name for his

protagonist. Without a name he didn't exist and could simply disappear, leaving no trace. He had to pin him down.

It mustn't be a contrived name, not a name suggesting some deeper meaning. No plays on words. No allusions to people who actually existed. Nothing like that.

In his previous books, he had used only first names – that had been enough. Perhaps, to start with, a letter would suffice. He thought X was too corny, Y ridiculous, Z too Hollywood. Just as Tereza started choking on her coffee, it came into his head, perfectly formed: I'll call him T.

It was a thought as clear as a voice.

I'll call him T, without a full stop; I don't have a name yet, so there's no name to abbreviate. T sounds pretty self-sufficient anyway. K's better, but not an option, not with that connotation. And the rest are no good. Can't exactly call him U. Or I. So, for now, I'll just call him T. Plain and simple.

"Put your arms in the air, Mummy!"

"I'm just going upstairs to note something down."

Her eyes streaming from her almighty coughing fit, Tereza gave him a surprised look. Now? While she was choking?

"Hands up, sweetheart."

In his office he removed the cover from the Olympia SG1, the Rolls-Royce of typewriters, built in 1959, 15 kilograms, purchased for 10 euros from the son of a war veteran who'd written a periodical on it for forty years. A typewriter was like an anvil or a shoemaker's last: it made him feel like he was mastering a craft. He inserted a virginal sheet of paper and typed a capital T.

He noted how the horizontal line ended on both sides with a long vertical stick that hung down to form a roof, shielding the letter from its surroundings. This letter might have been made for his protagonist.

Smiling, Steegman leaned back into the sheepskin.

He hammered a few Ts onto the paper.

Those eaves, set in a modern typeface, would most likely disappear in his book. But by then they would have served their purpose. They were of no concern to the reader. It mattered only to him, the writer, that everything was just right. Besides, T would get a real name in his book.

Downstairs, Tereza was waiting for him with Renée, ready to leave. Tereza worked in the city. Human resources. She had flexible working hours, but it was always Steegman who took Renée to the village school – he worked at home. Tereza was really good with people, could get anyone to do anything and, what's more, in a way that made them like her. Her command, her undivided attention.

It was a talent that Steegman lacked entirely. Even if his request was friendly, he still had the impression that people thought a scary man was harassing them. It had a lot, if not everything, to do with facial features, timbre and some indefinable softness in and around the eyes, sparingly and capriciously granted by nature. It wasn't an absence of these characteristics that had led him to start writing, but it was certainly a happy coincidence. He worked alone, at home.

For many people, working at home was an enviable "luxury": a word like a muzzle, imposing silence about his enforced existence as a house husband. He put the laundry in the washing machine and hung it out to dry, loaded the dishwasher, raked, wiped, polished, mowed, ironed, went to the baker's, to the chemist's, the butcher's, looked after Renée when she was ill, took care of the chickens, did the vacuuming, cleared up, and unloaded the dishwasher. During office hours. Then he cooked the dinner. Women's magazines would call him a new man, an appalling irony: Steegman had been born old-fashioned. But an old-fashioned wife, one who permitted him to be completely old-fashioned in all aspects of family life, would bore him to death. A proud thought that he carried with him all day long like a Swiss Army knife.

Steegman gave Tereza a kiss and waved goodbye to her backside as she headed down the garden path.

He would give T a wife just like that. In those trousers, black with a crease; hips and buttocks tenderly enclosed by the fabric, retaining its shape beautifully and yet free to move with her as she walks. She never wears jeans, T doesn't like them. Jeans are a suit of armour, very practical for some women – just as the stench of air freshener is practical in a busy lavatory. His wife does not go out to work. They lead a rather secluded life. He should give T a bestseller, one book in his oeuvre that has continued to sell over the years, internationally, in increasing numbers. A story that appeals to generation after generation of young readers, allegorical but accessible, nothing elitist about it. Winning all the prizes that matter, or perhaps not, a generally acknowledged disgrace. A book like *Animal Farm* or *Lord of the Flies*. An adventure story with unique depth, a book with which everyone can identify, road sweeper or vicar, something for everyone, always relevant, because the focus is on human nature and current events go unmentioned. The book's success allows T to ignore the media. The publication of his books is a literary event, particularly because he hardly publishes anything nowadays. His last interview was twenty years ago – eighteen: sounds more precise. On that occasion he got up halfway through the conversation and left, in the middle of an answer, in the middle of a sentence, which has since been thoroughly dissected and is referred to in every article about his work. The journalist has sold the famous interview, recorded on a T.D.K. cassette tape, to a literary museum, or a major art dealer, or an eccentric fan, for a ridiculous amount of money, maybe as much as 80,000 euros. He was getting sidetracked. First a title for this bestseller. He was about to bring out *The Murderer*, so T would perhaps have written *The Suspect*, or *The Guard*. One joke was surely permitted, one nod. A little extra seasoning. Writers were entertainers too, weren't they?

Steegman felt fingers fumbling at his hand. Pausing halfway out of the front door, he stared at the empty garden path and felt Renée wriggling her hand into his. It wasn't that she was subtly trying to make the point that they needed to leave right away if they didn't want to arrive late at school. Her concept of time was limited to "now" and "one more sleep", as straightforward as a fairy tale. No, her action was without any force or urgent message. Perhaps she thought he needed comforting, as he was still looking at the garden path, which Tereza had only just walked down. He was not alone.

Her hand was glowing with health; a new little hand, with bright blood in fine veins beneath pristine skin.

She didn't let go of him until they were in the garden. The expanse of the lawn always had the same effect on her: she ran. Right at the bottom, hidden between two fat conifers, was a gate that opened onto a path leading to the street with the village school. When they were living in the city, Steegman used to shuffle around the ring road for three quarters of an hour every morning to get to the nursery, and then half an hour back to his office, where, after ten minutes searching for a parking place, it would take him an hour to recover from the resulting urges to kill someone.

He closed the door of the sunroom and immediately heard the greenfinches, the blue tits, the robin, a dunnock, a blackcap with, beneath it all, the beautiful melancholy of a blackbird. It was like stepping into a warm, soothing bath. Although the garden had the atmosphere of a park, rather than the dimensions, it always delighted Steegman. He loved how the old slabs, sunk into the grass, gently meandered towards the conifers, their surface texture reminding him of his grandma's shortbread, and how Renée jumped from one to the next, as if crossing a wild river.

She was wearing his favourite outfit today. Skinny jeans with frayed hems below the knees, faded on the thighs and bum, kind of cool-looking, a sixteen-year-old girl in miniature. The pink anorak with its short, turned-up collar went surprisingly well with the jeans, especially because the cuffs were always undone. White sneakers completed the look. Renée was completely unaware of her appearance, and how affectionate she made her father feel.

So here he was, on this spring morning, walking in his own garden, with silver birch, magnolia and beech, with privet, creepers and cherry laurel, willow, reeds and jasmine. No one could see him, he was free from the gaze of strangers. He was alone with his own happiness, which had crystallised out of the ethereal and unfathomable and into the skipping figure before him. The gleam of her chestnut-brown hair – yes, chestnut-brown! The apple-round cheeks in her jeans. A rested and washed and cherished girl, beautiful, blissful, safe, in this precious moment, when he, Emiel Steegman, was freely and fully Emiel Steegman.

And yet a biographer in the one book that purports to present a portrait of his life, penetrating to his deepest essence, would not describe this moment. No biographer would ever walk here and feel what he was feeling now, or be capable of imagining it. That was impossible.

Renée tugged with both hands and all her strength at the bolt of the wrought-iron gate, which had been consumed by rust. When she stepped aside, Steegman pretended he too had to make a concerted effort to shift the bolt. He warned her first to look left and right for any cyclists; Renée ran blindly onto the path.

He would have to give T not only his wife, but also his daughter. This moment in his garden. This is where it could all begin. This is where he has the insight that sends his life in a new direction, the start of the novel. Unlike Steegman, T is a success. He never receives invitations to entertain unknown Estonian writers in some castle or other. If he did, he would flatly refuse and not put himself in an awkward position, because – you never knew how something might be of benefit – he always says yes first. And so he never has to come up with an excuse in the shower, with shampoo in his eyes, a simple little phrase that sets him thinking and doesn't let him go. Besides, shampoo stinging his eyes, a forty-year-old man? Beginning the book with such fussiness would cause even seasoned readers to sigh deeply.

The walk from the sunroom to the gate between the two conifers: nothing else would happen in the first chapter. Writer takes his daughter to school, the route is through his garden, it is spring. Still, the chapter would acquire a mythic scope. With its deceleration of time bordering on stasis, its wealth of effective detail, its captivating narrative. It would have all the intensity of the description of the third and final day of Ahab's battle with Moby Dick.

In his mind, he closed the sunroom door again, turned to face the garden. Where to begin? The scent. Of course! He would start with the smell of the little brewery in the village, wafting over his garden on the breeze. What was it called again? De Rijckere? De Rijcke. Or was it De Rijck? That peculiar odour, yeast or malt, what was it? Warm and appetising, like freshly baked bread. A scent as welcoming as a mother's hug. He could look it up later to find out exactly what it was.

What else?

Perhaps the trembling of thousands of birch leaves. The gentle clucking of the chickens. Tomorrow he would walk around the garden with a notebook and zoom in. Renée's narrow little shoulders, the chestnut brownness, the apple roundness, the way she runs with her arms barely moving, like Tereza; he would write it all down. He wouldn't have to state T's happiness – it would be obvious. Readers will instantly surrender and identify with T. They will feel welcome, want to stay. They will want to live in the prose, for as long as possible and at every moment of the day. Particularly at the end of the chapter, when T, just after his insight about his future biography, reaches the gate, and it's rusty, the perfect symbol of mortality, an ominous foreshadowing of his expulsion from paradise.

Steegman cheerfully kicked a pebble. A rusty gate. He could never have come up with that so quickly! It felt like a divine blessing of his new novel. His idea had immediately taken root in reality and would bear fruit. He realised that this important moment, too, the genesis of the first chapter, would not be chronicled by any biographer.

On the left, at the end, or perhaps the beginning, of one of the long, narrow gardens, a woman stood watching him. He could make out a laundry basket at her feet, her hands were on her hips, a beautiful, slender woman, he could clearly see that, even from a hundred metres away. He waved. The woman stood motionless. As if she too were surprised by his action. Then she yelled something. Halfway between them, a dog emerged from behind a low hutch, which probably contained rabbits.

Her posture exuding boredom, Renée waited for her father. Although the school was nearby, she kept to the agreement that she would stop and wait when she reached the pavement.

As Steegman walked towards her, the realisation fully hit him: for the first time, he was planning to use his own life as material for a book. Not out of vanity or laziness, as sometimes happened with other writers, but because it was more appropriate than ever. T's success didn't pose a problem; over a number of years Steegman had honed his ability to imagine success. The problem came from another quarter: he was by no means an expert on the life of Emiel Steegman. Never before, when writing a novel, had he focused on his own life. It played no part at all. He was a fiction writer, and therefore best served by a clear vision of his story, rather than being bombarded by memories, cluster bombs that exploded as soon as he sat down at his desk and dared to look out of the window.

Steegman's lack of memories was perhaps his one real talent. He had proudly proclaimed it in many an interview, it was his answer to the inevitable question about the autobiographical content of his work. He was free. He felt as light as a hummingbird buzzing from one colourful flower to the next and did not, thank God, stand around endlessly ruminating behind barbed wire like a cow surrounded by its own excrement. He created, and because he shaped his imagination to suit his story, his books were streamlined and precise. The writer was nowhere to be found, he was as invisible as Jean-Baptiste Grenouille in the legendary bestseller *Perfume*. Grenouille has no smell of his own and steals other people's scents so as to be seen and loved, just as Steegman does with the lives of his characters.

He didn't know why he had so few memories. Did he find it difficult to make them, or was he forgetful? Lazy perhaps, or indifferent? Or were his memories trapped somewhere, piled up in their thousands, with only the occasional one managing to escape? Would science, if he'd been born fifty years later, be able to locate the fault

41

in his brain, a local spot of bother between a handful of neurons, responsible for his literary quirk?

Renée had seen that her teacher was helping the children to cross the road today, and she was skipping impatiently. He took hold of her outstretched hand.

No, he thought. It wasn't indifference.

He'd recently watched a YouTube clip of Johnny Cash, an interview from fifteen, twenty years ago, recounting memory after memory of his schooldays, more years ago than Steegman had lived. First names, surnames. When he closed his eyes for a moment, only one bubble rose up from the depths of the swamp. He is sixteen. Secondary school, maths. The grey 1980s, shapeless jumpers, ageing varnish on old school desks. At break time, dying of boredom, four of them hiding from the drizzle. Beside the hanging bike racks, one up, one down, Karel takes out an intensely green apple, sinks all his teeth into it. The first time it's simply hilarious: the whack, the surprise factor, the apple flying into the air, Karel scrambling away – a movement like stumbling, without hope, an overture to the inevitable. When it happens again a little later, it's beyond laughter, it's struggling to breathe, bent double, bellies grasped, greyness gone; foolish hysteria. And then it's over. When Steegman hits, he can feel it even as the apple leaves Karel's fingers. Disapproval. No-one thinks it's funny anymore. The apple spins through the air without Karel looking at it or grabbing for it, that beautiful apple, soon to be bruised and filthy. He'd like to catch it himself, but that's not an option. He cannot rectify his mistake, he cannot turn back the clock. He wants to apologise, but that's not an option either, as now he needs to put Karel in a headlock because he's being attacked. Has to force him to his knees, hurt him, humiliate him, even though he knows it'll be weeks before the close-knit gang of friends is the same again.

Steegman remembered summoning that memory before. Just that one. Six years of secondary school reduced to a single instance of poor judgement.

Other people must be better at remembering. He'd been alive for forty years now; how many other people's memories must he feature in? How many impressions had he left, the existence of which he could suspect, but not exactly what they entailed or who had hung onto them . . . ?

Renée called out to her teacher; she didn't hear her, standing with arms wide in the middle of the road, her back to them. She was wearing a fluorescent tabard, light-blue jeans. Fifteen metres separated them. Steegman felt as if he'd just woken up on a snow-white beach, spat out by the raging surf on the desert island of his own life. With rising excitement, he walked towards the adventure, which would begin in a few seconds in the teacher's eyes, where Steegman would catch a glimpse of Renée's father.

6

Andy appears on his bike, standing upright on the pedals, his saddle whipping back and forth. Just in front of Emiel, he slams on the brakes, the back wheel throwing up sand and dust as it swings out.

A great big lorry, he says. Parked outside his house, with the engine running. The man in the cab is speaking to some other men through a microphone with a curly cable. A transmitter, he's talking into a transmitter, because there's a long antenna on the roof. Andy says he could hear it all, the window was open. An orange lorry, but a really dirty one, especially at the back, like a chicken's bum or a sheep's, covered with black gunk. And it stinks. It stinks so bad you can hardly breathe. Andy asks what Emiel's eating. Is he eating cherries? The cherries on his grandmother's tree never get really red, or soft. Or sweet. Did his mum buy the cherries?

They ride their bikes next to each other, Emiel half a wheel in front. Jürgen's already there, Petra too. The driver's elbow's sticking out of the window, he's talking into the microphone, listening to the buzzing, the crackling voices, and then he reaches out his arm and taps the ash from his cigarette. He thinks it's only natural for children to cluster around his lorry. He laughs when Jürgen shouts "America?" above the noise of the radio. He puts his head out of the window, a whole storey high, and says, "Overvelde." Overvelde, a district of Zingene. Andy lets out a squeal: he's pulling carefully at some dry skin that's peeling off his sunburnt thigh, but the strip of skin quickly narrows to a point and breaks off. He needs to be more patient, says Petra. She plucks skin from his shoulders with her fingernails. Jürgen asks if they can hear him in America. Or is his antenna too short?

Jürgen and Petra are twelve, were in the same class until this summer. Andy's the youngest, he's almost eleven, a muscular boy with short legs and white-blond hair, and coarse facial features, in which hints of the ugly adult man can already be seen. A live wire. When he runs, he always runs as fast as he can, chin high, fists up, until, exhausted, he drops down on the ground as if he's dead. After Emiel's promise of silence, after he crossed his heart, after he spat between his index finger and middle finger, Petra says her mum told her that she heard from Andy's mum that he still sleeps with the light on at night. Sometimes he has a little accident.

After that announcement, they sit together, deep in thought. It's just before the summer holidays, a Saturday, late afternoon. Soon he'll have to go home, go to Mass with his mum. Petra knows what she means about Andy's "accidents". He knows too, almost, the expression isn't entirely unfamiliar, the light, the accident, the connection; he can't really concentrate. There's another matter for urgent attention: the silence, which presses very close in the small camp that Petra made all on her own. The ground is cold, the heat hasn't yet penetrated into the

45

maize field. In the distance, along a track between the stalks, he sees bright light splashing off the white sand. Left and right, only stalks, a remote part of the field, some way from the big camp. He is a guest, they've ridden their bikes to one of the last streets on the new estate, Petra hid her bike in the maize and told him to do the same. She wanted to keep her place a secret from the others. Perhaps she doesn't mind his silence, but he still owes it to her to speak. He thinks about the big camp, how easy it is there, with the others around, talking to her about this and that. Perhaps she's regretting it already. Maybe she's thinking: this isn't what he wanted. Or: my nose is too big.

"Jürgen fancies me." She gives a deep sigh, wraps her arms around her tucked-up knees, her hair is hiding her face.

He thinks she has a beautiful nose. It really doesn't matter that it's big. This isn't about her nose. But he can't say that, because she'll think the opposite.

She picks up a stone and draws white lines on the taut, brown instep of her right foot. The skin on her arm wrinkles, the hairs stand on end. The longest ones touch the curly hairs on his leg.

She has a wonderful nose.

7

The apron, which belonged to Arlette, his neighbour across the road, was covered with a profusion of un-identifiable flowers. He had plenty of time to look at them. Voluptuous calyxes with dramatic petals and over-grown stamens. Probably an artist's impression. The apron hung from a solitary plastic hook, the rest of the sunroom's only actual wall was whitewashed and empty. In his novel, Arlette would wear the flowers every day, even when vis-itors came, or under her coat at the supermarket.

She was nowhere in sight, she must be upstairs doing something important that she couldn't abandon. François had already called her name twice from the hallway and, without waiting for an answer – because his wife was at home, he was sure of that – he'd closed the door again and hurried to the visitors in the sunroom. "She's coming."

The man was in his early seventies and he was part of the street's scenery, just like Lodewijk. As soon as the weather permitted, he lived outside, keeping close to his house. His wife, though, to the best of Steegman's knowledge, never left the building. Unlike Lodewijk, François wasn't a keen gardener. He didn't seem to have the patience for it. He didn't garden, he *worked* in the garden. If he wasn't doing that, he'd be up to something with a hammer or a drill, or climbing the ladder again and waving hello as he balanced on the gutter or sat astride the roof. When there were no more jobs to be done, not even at his widowed neighbour's, he unfolded his deck-chair in front of the garage and, limbs spread wide, feet bare, eyes devoutly shut, he worshipped the sun.

On that day in early spring, wearing a green pair of Adidas shorts from the 1970s and a pair of flip-flops, as bronzed as a Spaniard, he was sitting in the shady sun-room, where, according to the digital thermometer stuck to what had once been the outside window of the house, it was 15.8 degrees Celsius, with 78 per cent humidity. No matter where Steegman looked, he couldn't shake the image of those hardened, elongated nipples that, with François' every movement, seemed to dangle from his broad chest like a pair of listless worms. He was ready to distract Renée before she noticed and started asking questions.

Because there were no other distractions in the sunroom. A sagging leather sofa and a dresser with three cacti on saucers. The thermometer (or was it a weather station?) and the apron on a hook. The size of the neighbours' tree meant the shade in the sunroom must be permanent.

Steegman had been walking back with Renée from the playground by the crossing at the bottom of the street when they'd bumped into François. As always, his greeting had been unusually warm. Just as when they'd first met, he'd taken Renée's face in his hands and regarded her with a silent smile. That first time Steegman had thought: he's going to kiss her. François had squatted down, his left thumb stroking her eyebrow. If he kisses her, let it be on her forehead, on her cheek, don't let him kiss my daughter on the lips. He stood by, watching helplessly, the man was doing nothing wrong, was just showing a little affection. Time had condensed, became as thick as caramel, as he searched the face of this man, François, a man he'd never seen before, as if both Renée's life and his own depended on it, every wrinkle, the tension in his nostrils, the reflection on the glassy white of the man's eye (a roof on the other side of the street, with the clear sky behind), so as not to miss any sign of a change for the sinister. If he dares to kiss her on the lips, thought Steegman, I'm going to shove him over and kick him senseless. He thought: keep your paws off my daughter, you old bastard, and he felt his own smile freeze on his face. He watched the scene from a distance: nothing seemed to be wrong. He cursed himself, he should have intervened at once, always as meek as a lamb, always the chief witness to his own fate, guilty by omission. Just one more movement, he resolved, and yet there was the vision of the fear and distress in his daughter's eyes, after her daddy had finished going crazy and that nice man who had given her a kiss was lying lifeless on his perfectly surfaced driveway, bleeding from his nose and mouth.

Then François said what he'd said that afternoon, what he always said: "Come on in. Then Arlette can say hello, too."

Today Steegman hadn't rejected his suggestion out of hand, had left a strategic pause, more than enough encouragement for him to start leading Renée round to the back of the house, to the sunroom, taking little steps, slightly bending his knees, leaning over to hold tightly on to her hand as if she were made of porcelain.

The coffee was ready. François handed him a cup and asked if he took sugar. He brought a sugar lump out of the pocket of his Adidas shorts, wrapped in well-thumbed and tattered paper. Horses, he explained. He always took a sugar lump with him for the horses when he went for a walk across the field. No, replied Steegman. No sugar.

Black.

François was holding up the sugar lump between his fingers now, like a magician, as if he'd just conjured it out of nowhere, right under Renée's nose. "Your daddy says it's allowed, just this once." He tore open the paper, corners and edges crumbling. As Renée looked from the grey pebble in her palm up at her father, a question on her face, a mass of water went gushing through the bowels of the house. It crashed down, in a sudden burst, before the noise travelled onwards, racing away. Then the sound of footsteps, already very close.

First he saw her arm, reaching through the kitchen door for the apron, and then in a single motion Arlette stepped into the sunroom, hung the apron around her neck and tied the ribbon around her waist, before even glancing at the guests.

The woman looked like most other females of her age. Hairstyle, glasses, shoes, figure; barely distinguishable from one another. Sometimes he saw them being guided around in groups, all on identical bikes.

"I said to Emiel, I said, why don't you pop round with Renée. Say hello to Arlette. It's been too long."

Steegman said hello, introduced himself as a neighbour from across the road, but received no response. When Arlette set eyes on Renée, she brought her hand to her mouth. The other hand flew to her chest. As she opened her mouth wide, her glasses slipped to the tip of her nose.

"Arlette," said François.

"What a beautiful little girl, Mr Steegman," she said finally. It was just above a whisper.

"Thank you. Please call me Emiel."

Arms open wide, Arlette inched closer to Renée. It looked like she was trying to catch an escaped chicken. Renée made a little noise and cuddled up to her dad.

"But, sweetheart," said François. "There's no need to be scared of Arlette. Arlette's really nice to little children, didn't you know that?" He ruffled Renée's hair. "Arlette just wants to feel how soft your hair is and how soft your little cheeks are. That's all. Grown-ups like that kind of thing. Arlette won't hurt you, she really loves children. She's never, ever hurt a little kiddy."

Arlette stopped at the point her shuffling steps had reached. She put her hands on her thighs and leaned forward. "It's only natural," she said, "for Renée to be a little bit frightened. You just hush now. You're only making it worse."

"She's not frightened," said François. "She's not frightened of you, Arlette, she doesn't know you: that's not the same thing. She's just not used to us. Why should children be frightened of you? You're a woman like any other woman. You could be her granny."

The word "granny" had a strange effect on her. Her smile crumpled, her eyes went flat, until finally they were just staring, at Renée.

"Shall I tell you something, Renée?" said François. "Arlette looked after a little kiddy for a while, who used to call her 'Granny Arlette', as if she really were her grandma. So Arlette knows everything there is to know about little children like you, she has lots and lots of experience. And she's very nice. So there's no need for you to be frightened."

After a brief silence in which no-one moved, François turned to speak to Steegman, in hushed tones, an aside from man to man. "With the technology they have nowadays, it would have been a different story. Then it would have worked – the gynaecologist said so. Everything's different now, he said. The impossible has become possible – those are *his* words. We didn't need the impossible, but back then hardly anything was possible." He ruffled Renée's hair, stroked her cheek with the back of his hand. "And you're really not related?"

"Related?"

"Wiet said you're not related. To the baker."

"The previous owners? No, we're not related."

"No," said François. "Remarkable."

"No," said Steegman. "What Lodewijk told us was the first we'd heard of it."

"Two peas in a pod." François sank into the armchair and turned away from Renée. He could look out one side of his sunroom and see Steegman's house. He always sat in this chair; the distance was far enough that they didn't have to wave when Steegman glanced through the window and saw François sitting in the sunroom, facing in his direction.

"Do you know the worst part? They never did find little Vicky. Poor girl."

"Who's Vicky?" Steegman realised he was stroking Renée's hair so hard he was almost pulling it.

"Hot chocolate. Arlette used to make buckets of it. With real chocolate. And waffles, my goodness. Long ago, Emiel, but never over. That's what my aunt said whenever she thought back to her childhood, in the First World War. Long ago, but never over."

"My aunt," said Arlette. "Julia."

"The first time I saw little Renée, I nearly fell over." He took a deep breath and looked thoughtfully at his wife. "Twenty-two. How old would Vicky be now?"

"Twenty-two," said Arlette.

8

T is sitting in the garden. Or he's sitting in his study, day-dreaming in the rippling haze of the net curtain. Perhaps he's lying beside his little daughter in her big canopy bed. A double bed with a mosquito net, she's frightened, of monsters and ghosts, but mainly of thieves, who are going to take everything that's precious to her, starting with Bear, her cuddly toy since she was born, a limp, brown rag with two round ears, looking laconically through his scratched eyes, Mummy and Daddy too, of course, but the first thing the thieves will make off with, what they're most interested in, is Bear, an intolerable thought that made her cry, silently at first, the kind of crying that sometimes stops by itself, but which turned into sobs this evening, culminating in her yelling at the top of her voice, about Daddy this time, panicking about Daddy, who might already have been stolen. In his hand he feels her consciousness ebbing away, he feels the brain sending small, uncontrolled signals to the muscles in her forearm, which tug at the tendons in her fingers. He goes on lying there for a little longer, alone with his thoughts in this haven, in the cosy, red glow of the toadstool lamp with its little holes that sprinkle stars across the ceiling and pink wall-paper. In this fairy tale, he once again ponders a sentence he recently read in the biography of famous thriller writer Patricia Highsmith. A sentence in the introduction to the book, from a letter to a friend: "I do NOT mean to sound as important as Winston Churchill, but am absolutely sure someone will wish to 'write something' when I'm dead."

T is standing in the garden. The wind, or maybe a cat, has knocked over the zinc bucket, the grass beneath it is dead. A place where Renée never goes, so why bother putting the bucket away every time? Always on the first day of a new month, for thirteen years now, after walking out in the middle of an interview, in the middle of a sentence. A place beyond the reach of even the most attentive neighbour, who at dinner that evening mentions the strange smell of burning, calendar in hand, as his wife nods and asks if he wants more gravy. The dark-brown sludge has trickled over the edge, disappeared into the lawn, fertiliser. He has less and less to burn these days. He has very little correspondence with anyone. Just one true friend has solemnly promised to do the same. He trusts him, he wants to be able to trust him. Notes, draft versions, he doesn't hang on to them for any longer than a month. After a month they need to have been transformed into lasting prose. He takes his time, sitting on a folding chair, doesn't light the next sheet of paper until the previous one has been entirely consumed by the flames. Sometimes the acrid smoke billows into his face, he inhales, savours it, trying to forget the countless painful examples over the years that have proved him right. A great writer dies and a collection of his file cards covered with scraps of writing is posthumously presented as a novel, the promotional hubbub overshadowing his actual work – an insult. Last wills and testaments are trampled underfoot by grasping publishers and greedy heirs in the interests of the greater literary good. A book of letters is unashamedly given the title *"Rip up this Letter!"*, complete with exclamation mark – a quote. T savours the scent of the smoke as if he were smoking a cigarette. But in his closed eyes he can still see throngs of people charging into the wings, blind to the carefully lit action on the stage.

Not thirteen years ago, but nine. It is summer in the city, the door of the café is open. T is recognised, hears the whispers of polite people conspicuously doing their best not to see him. He is not friends with the journalist, but he is an old acquaintance, favourably disposed since his debut, without falling at his feet. He thinks it would be impolite to make the man join all the other journalists in the lobby of some swanky hotel. A cosy café, a summer afternoon. Through the doorway he has a full-length view of the women passing by, flimsy dresses swirling around their long, smooth legs, the gleam of round shoulders. Now and then a delicate hint of flowers wafts inside, dispelling the bitterness of coffee. He feels a twinge of pain, at not being one of them; carefree, simply knowing oneself to be admired. He hears himself talking, in weighty tones because of the recording, a concatenation of words chaining down his helpless novel, restricting its movement. It dawns on him that what he says has gradually become more important than what he has written. As soon as the idea takes hold of him that he's actually free to stand up and leave the café, it is not a crime, the chair legs scrape across the tiled floor and he disappears through the open door and into the city. What happens after that will astound T; yes, it will astound him, but in a way it will also confirm to him that he is right: the news that this journalist has sold the cassette to the highest bidder. An annual salary for half a sentence. A child or a grandchild in need. An unreasonable wife. Accident, illness. A 1974 caramel-coloured Porsche. The astonishment and the confirmation are followed by an insane cackle. An incomplete sentence will probably be his most famous one, an epitaph, spoken absent-mindedly, already outside in the sunshine, seven words with no significance. Followed by another four minutes of sounds from the café. The journalist, or so he reads later, thinks T has recognised someone out on the street and popped out to say hello, and that he'll be back soon, and will sit down and carry on talking; four minutes and eleven seconds later, he changes his mind and stops the recording. Unaware of his unborn grandson's accident. Unaffected by any obsession with classic sports cars.

T is sitting on a teak garden bench. In the cellar. T's house has a basement that runs the entire length of the house, an extra floor containing the garage and other rooms. In one of those rooms is the garden bench, which was never taken back upstairs after one winter, years ago. The garden has no shortage of benches. This room is where the clothes are washed, foaming suds slosh around inside the washing machine. A line is strung above his head, his daughter's summer dresses, motionless. He is surrounded by cables, insulated pipes, a low humming that indicates activity. He sees couplings, he sees taps, he thinks about heavy industry and chimneys, about storage depots with forklift trucks, wholesalers' with fraying flags, he thinks about a van with writing on the side, the plumber in his blue overalls; he thinks about how all of that has come together in this little corner under the ground, a focal point, his little corner, where he retreats, drinks a bottle of beer, listens to sport, feels safe. Where he believes he's escaping the world.

Opposite, on the concrete shelves that aren't filled with bottles of wine, are cardboard boxes of complimentary copies of the translations and reprints of his work. Everything he has made public, sent out into the world. But if he dies tomorrow, it won't be enough. As soon as his life comes to an end, no story will be more eagerly anticipated than the story of his own life. In an age when revelation is the highest currency, when people long for the acknowledgement of the stranger on the other side of the medium, his unshakable silence has become exotic. His biography will be advertised as "revealing", "fascinating"; commercial success will be guaranteed, a story that literary readers, libraries and bookshops will artificially add to his oeuvre, a key, *the* explanation, the first and ultimately the only book people reach for when they think of T, the only one in the series that he, with the exception of the beginning and the ending, the dates of his birth and death, has nothing to do with at all. Everything in between, everything he has so carefully deleted, withheld and burned, someone equally determined will fill in the gaps, as he sees fit, with the authority of someone who was there himself.

T is forty-five years old. He has a daughter, she is called Renée. She is asleep. In the red glow of her nightlight he stares at the stars on the ceiling. His head is resting on his arm, his legs are crossed at the ankles, her little finger and ring finger occasionally twitch in his hand. He can't hear anything. Not a dog in the distance, not a car. Nothing. He tries his hardest, but he gets stuck at his fifth birthday, somewhere in the countryside, pigpens in the background, the stench of manure, wild grass in an endless garden, and him on a plastic tractor, a yellow tractor with red wheels and a red seat and a red steering wheel, a present. He's probably remembering the photograph. He's soaked up the saturated colours of the Polaroid, a slow and unconscious process, no longer distinguishable from actual recall.

T has a daughter, Renée; she is nearly four. If he dies tomorrow, she will retain hardly any memories of her father. She'll soak up the story that other people have made about him.

and clearly has nothing to do with it all. Everything in
everyone, everything, he is specifically deluded with all
and I'm not, someone equally deluded almost will all in the
perfectly at ease with the reality by someone who is
there himself.

9

At the D.I.Y. store, Steegman bought a spade and a large
hand shovel. He joined the queue of hulking men in work
gear at the till. They smelled honest, of bricks or wood,
with an underlying note of tobacco, or endearingly of
something tough and manly from a supermarket bottle.
One by one, they paid with banknotes, arranged in order
of value inside bulging wallets that they pulled from their
back pockets at the last moment; one by one, they were
greeted by a mosaic of wife and children.

They would certainly be able to pick him out in a
line-up: tall, slim, blond, glasses, jacket and smart shoes,
standing there awkwardly with his spade and his shovel,
smiling strangely at them, exactly the profile of a deranged
individual who doesn't stop for a moment to consider that
his appearance might make people wonder what in God's
name he's planning to do with that spade and shovel.

On his way back, he saw the pickup parked halfway
on the pavement in front of his house. They were early.
He could, of course, have asked the gardener if he might
borrow a spade and shovel, the man must have enough
to spare, but this way was better, this way he could be
sure. He was showing that he was serious; he wasn't the
kind of man to do a job by halves. He'd taken care to

buy not the cheapest, but not the most expensive either, a safe choice, which would spare him the silent scorn of the professionals.

Steegman drove into his garage, came back out with the tools, leaned them against the wall, and walked around the side of the house and into the garden. The three men were working away, getting ready to start the trimming. He produced no sound on the lawn, so Steegman coughed to get their attention before he actually reached them. The boss, whom he'd already met for a quote, immediately stood up straight: two metres of glowing health, a handshake that was a little timid and therefore appealing. The other two men were at least ten years older, but still younger than Steegman. They stood shoulder to shoulder, nodded and then watched him a little vacantly, like sheep with a dog. The oldest one, the baldest one, had one sticking-out ear. One sticking-out ear was most definitely worse than two.

Steegman knew that in this kind of situation he had to observe certain customs and courtesies to ensure the work went as smoothly as possible, but he had no idea what those customs and courtesies might be. Three gardeners, that was new to him. Besides, they'd only just got there, hadn't even started work. Wouldn't it be odd, fussy, if he offered them coffee right away? Or would it make them feel welcome, like guests, and therefore morally obliged not to disappoint their host under any circumstances? Coffee? For hardworking outdoor men on a sunny day in springtime? Beer seemed more appropriate. He couldn't do it now, no-one would dare to accept, and it would make a strange impression, thinking it was normal to

61

start drinking so early. Later, in a few hours. He pictured himself sitting in the shade on the grass, on his backside, not squatting, the men on their coolbox, each with a glistening bottle in his hand, little jokes, easy laughter, a look at the sky, the sound of glugging at their lips, yes, beer would make him one of them, a man for whom, a quarter of an hour later, they would be prepared to work as if it were their own garden. But maybe they'd think the mere assumption that they'd drink alcohol at work was an insult: they were expensive, conscientious professionals, not Polish cowboys on some illegal building site!

Rattled by the awkwardly swelling silence, Steegman said, "Good luck, then." As one, the men bent down to the ground. Three seconds later it would have sounded different, unpleasant, as if he had little faith that this taciturn trio could handle his garden. He waited until he was almost out of sight, then turned and shouted that if they needed him they could find him round at the front. It seemed genuine, casual. A brief affirmative sound came from two of the men.

Down in the basement, in the laundry, he put on old clothes. A light-blue shirt and jeans. What he always wore, in fact. No-one would notice the difference between his work clothes and his ordinary clothes, he would have to point it out. Once he was in his muddy wellingtons, he summoned up courage again and walked out through the garage into the sunlight, a gladiator entering the arena, his weapons a spade and a shovel.

The distance from the house to the gas pipe under the pavement was a little more than the length of a car. The driveways were separated by a lost patch of ground, a square, outlined by old-fashioned, uneven concrete slabs. In the middle, on a sturdy pedestal, a garden ornament, a fountain at first glance, but actually a simple basin with a cherub playing the lyre or showering itself with water from a pitcher – after decades in wind and weather, it could have been either. He looked at the knee-high wall beside the pavement and hoped he wouldn't hit any over-grown foundations. Hidden behind the wall, on the half that belonged to the other house, was the mouldering post of the previous FOR SALE sign, which had blown away in an autumn storm and been lost for good.

Steegman picked up the shovel and began scooping away the layer of red gravel from the spot where he was planning to excavate, so that, later, when the energy sup-plier had made the connection, he could spread it back over the filled-in hole.

When he hit the first real obstruction, his breath caught in his throat. It was, of course, ridiculous. It was unthinkable. Last night he'd come to the conclusion that it had to be impossible. An hour of googling had revealed nothing about any "Vicky". No court case, no suspicious disappearance, no commotion. Halfway through an article about Vicky Leandros he'd decided to call it a day and went to bed. He didn't mention it to Tereza. If the girl had ever disappeared in alarming circumstances, then the police would have started by thoroughly searching these houses and the land they were built on. That was a fair assumption, wasn't it?

He kneeled down and wrenched the elongated object from the soil. Not the bleached bones of a child, but a rusty piece of iron.

"Construction waste," he heard above his head. "They used it to fill up the driveways and this piece of land."

Lodewijk had appeared sooner than Steegman expected.

The gas company always used to do everything themselves, he said. A trench, half a metre deep and half a metre wide, all the way to the pavement? He'd never heard anything like it. He pondered this for a long time, considering the question, hands deep in his big pockets, corners of his mouth turned down, shoulders hunched, eyes fixed on the ground in front of his feet: "No. Never." He affected the same posture when he walked; carrying the weight of the world on his shoulders, his hips creaking under the load, and yet still he – "Wiet" to his friends – cheerfully went on walking. Without any obvious transition, it would one day become his real old man's posture, just as the smells that have always surrounded a person suddenly and inevitably begin to reek of decline as they get older.

Steegman lifted the handle of the spade in front of his face and forcefully struck the blade into the ground, missing his own toes by just a few centimetres. The realisation of what he'd just escaped, in front of Lodewijk, made him break out in a cold sweat. He stuck the spade into the ground now and stood on one side of it, but couldn't keep his balance for long enough to drive the metal into the earth. Lodewijk turned away, left, then right, looked at the quiet street and the parked pickup.

He asked if they were going to prune the birch. Steegman knew birches grow really quickly and so they don't ever get old, didn't he? The tree had been there for fifty years, a long life for a birch. One strong gust of wind was all it took, could be lethal. Steegman replied that he'd asked the gardener to do whatever was needed, but before he could finish his sentence, Lodewijk yelled: "Pickaxe!" He was shouting to someone Steegman couldn't see. Lodewijk pointed down with an exaggerated gesture, "Construction waste! And the lad's struggling along with a spade."

While waiting, and feeling rather irritated by the word "lad", Steegman kept hacking away at the ground. He threw his entire body into the struggle. Until he hit a stone and the force of the impact painfully resonated from his fingertips to his tailbone.

Then he heard the flapping of flip-flops. Pickaxe on his shoulder, François looked at Steegman as if contemplating a traffic accident. For a few seconds it seemed as if he were going to step into the breach and relieve the suffering of the man with the slipping glasses and the soaked-through shirt. But Steegman wanted to make it perfectly clear: he, and no-one else, certainly not a man of over seventy, was going to dig this trench. That was the whole point. He had perhaps been a little lax in maintaining the garden, but when it really counted, when there was urgent digging work to be done, he was perfectly willing to roll up his sleeves and work himself into a lather of sweat. This man of words concealed a man of action.

Apparently he hadn't yet reached that point in Lodewijk's perception. "Lad." Perhaps meant in a fatherly way, but not likely. Steegman chopped the earth into loose piles, which he shovelled to one side. While the two men spoke in the local dialect, making themselves practically unintelligible, he considered what to do with the pair of them. Was there room for them in the book?

That depended on T. Does T have any contact with his neighbours? He lives in isolation, in the countryside, keeps his distance from the city and the literary scene, refusing every interview, but he's not a recluse. Taking on the role of the prickly hermit really would mean smugly embracing his status as a celebrated writer. He writes published books. He is a father and a husband. He wants to be in the flow of life, real life, he wants to play a part in Renée's world, Renée, who is given Smurf cards by the neighbour. Writer Smurfs.

How would Lodewijk react to his written likeness? Happy? Surprised? Proud? Shocked at the recognition? Perhaps Lodewijk would be deeply offended if he did *not* include him, but wrote instead about the more colourful François. Either way, if Steegman had a chance to talk to him about it afterwards, he would invoke the laws of the novel. The author's omnipotence was a fable, the story is dictated to him; with a straight face he would trot out phrases like that, sitting at the dining table and stirring a cup of coffee as he selects a biscuit from the assortment that the man's wife has arranged on a china plate, an almond finger, a nutty little biscuit, with the novel, the prime piece of evidence, lying on the lace tablecloth between him and Lodewijk.

He could not rule out the possibility that Lodewijk would read something about the book in the newspaper and then take a look purely out of curiosity about his neighbour, as a legitimate voyeur. François, on the other hand, seemed more like the type to flick through advertising leaflets at most. But his cameo role in the book would come to his attention sooner or later. He'd told the story about their wish for children, about Arlette's infertility, with a certain eagerness, as if he thought Steegman and Tereza wondered, on a daily basis, why the two of them had no children. A story that he told to everyone, always in muted tones and just between the two of us, because he was convinced they were all asking the same question. He wanted people to know it had not been their decision, that they were essentially no different from people with children, that he was a real man and Arlette a real mother.

Would it be indiscreet, amoral? Could he employ a scene, one that he'd normally devise with intense pleasure and great satisfaction, if it might later be thrown at him by a neighbour, sitting in the leather armchair in his sunroom, in the presence of his upset wife?

A new sound. His last thrust had made a strange thud. The two men peered down into the hole with him. Steegman brushed the soil from a wide, ceramic pipe, rust-brown. At this point he was not even thirty centimetres down. The sewage pipe, came the unanimous verdict. He'd only damaged the surface of the pipe: narrowly escaping grim fate for the second time.

But sadly that was not the end of the story. His back and arms were already worn out, for the next couple of days he wouldn't be able to get out of bed without Tereza's help, and now he would have to dig around the sewage pipe, mostly with his hands. His writer's hands. Sweat was dripping from his nose onto the pipe, faster and faster; the rust-brown, he could see it really close up, was turning blood-red.

His life was seeping out of him.

Then he felt his dejected expression transform into a smile.

Only then, he thought. Only then is it allowed. Only if rust-brown becomes blood-red. Otherwise I have to keep quiet about the neighbours.

10

It's as if the white kerbstones form the brick walls of a canal, filled with new tarmac, watery smoothness between maize and beets, with, at the end, a small black lake, where you can turn. A ribbon of red-and-white striped plastic still lingers. The lorries and the steamroller, the noise, the intruders have disappeared from the neighbourhood. Their realm is silent once again, clear and simple, theirs alone.

The lake is a seething swamp. From the roadside, Andy pierces a blister of tar with a branch. Jürgen throws a pebble, which is immediately seized by the blackness, without bouncing. Jürgen and Petra stand hand in hand – Petra is looking at him, Emiel; Jürgen at Andy. There's tension in the air, everyone can feel that the swamp must offer opportunities for entertainment.

They hear a bike bell. He recognises the bright-red bikini top, the pale shorts, the blonde hair pinned up. Sandra's a few months older than him. She's at a strict girls' school, uniform compulsory. She's freewheeling, has stopped pedalling, she's modestly holding her knees together. Usually she stays in the garden, with her little brother and her dad, his Mediterranean complexion as brown as his daughter's. The corners of her mouth gently turn up. She's always equally friendly to everyone who crosses her path, a cordon sanitaire, a fixed, safe distance. Her eyes are too dark to fathom.

A young cat jumps playfully out of the field of maize at the bike gliding past, a little tiger in white socks. Farmer Tuyt allows the first litter of the year to live, but not the second. It's easy for the cats to find food in the summer. By the next year, most of them have disappeared. Jürgen says the farmer puts the second litter in a potato sack and, when his wife's not around, he bashes them against the wall. His dad told him so. His dad helps with the harvest.

Sandra slowly brakes and carefully rides back. After laying down her bike on the new road surface, she sits down cross-legged, turning her back on the little tiger, which is standing on the edge, front legs bent, sniffing at the perfume of suntan lotion and acne cream. Andy tries to sabotage her plan by hissing and whooping, but he doesn't let him. His gaze wanders to the farm in the distance, an inward-looking complex of buildings and pens. Someone would only be able to watch them through one window at the top of the gable, at a very sharp angle.

Sandra strokes the little tiger. At first the animal seems to want to evade her hand by lithely bending its back, but then it discovers the pleasure, and wildly pushes up its head and back. This new-found confidence reminds it of its hunger, it meows for food, flashing its needle-sharp teeth. Sandra picks up the cat and hugs it to her chest, walks towards the others.

No-one has brought anything to eat. They're sitting in a circle on the ground, the little tiger running from one to the next, begging. Finally it tries to climb up Sandra and stabs a claw into the gleaming curve of her left breast. In a reflex reaction, she arches her spine and shoots backwards, her full, bright-red bikini swinging from her shoulders as never before, but she doesn't make a sound and the corners of her mouth are still gently upturned. She moistens her index finger with spit and strokes the wound. Andy laughs longest, awkwardly.

Jürgen says cats like to eat anything that's sweet. There's sugar in beets. He and Andy dig one up out of the field. They wipe the beet clean and then, after about five attempts, smash it into pieces on the kerbstone. The cat sniffs it, licks it, but doesn't take a bite. Dogs, he says. It's dogs that like sweet things. Cats are hunters. Even so, the pulp that he makes by bashing a chunk of beet with a stone seems to have tempted the cat. It laps greedily from his hand.

The excitement about the cat evaporates in the blazing sun. Until someone, Jürgen, throws a chunk of beet at the black swamp. The little tiger follows the projectile, ears pointed and back legs twitching, eager to hunt its prey. The stench of hot tarmac distracts him, makes him think again.

After that, it all happens quickly; the group dynamic kicks in. Andy, the youngest, the clown with the coarse features: he doesn't avoid any challenge that's ever whispered into his ear, any chance to prove himself a daredevil, to tease the unattainable girls, to force a laugh out of them, a squeal of pleasure or horror. He sees it as a sign of friendship when the oldest one tells him to do something, a duty. He, the quiet one, the observer, who uses Andy and his antics to assert his own authority as leader.

Petra cries out as Andy grabs hold of the cat, Sandra watches impassively, gently, her arms folded under the red bikini, as if she has known all along how this would play out, and now finally wants to see what happens, issuing her own challenge to the boys: show us what the two of you can do, go on.

Holding the animal at arm's length, Andy flings it like a hammer. The silence is complete, its flight is without a sound, no-one breathes, the tail swishes, instantly the white paws nimbly start seeking the ground. It only just makes the landing, the shock is absorbed by every joint, the stomach sinks deep, briefly touching the tarmac. For a second, nothing happens. The head is mid-turn towards the onlookers when suddenly the hindquarters are cata- pulted high into the air, with a force that makes the animal do a twisting somersault. In this new flight, screeching and wailing rises, fur stands on end, tail as thick as a fox's brush. The black ground refuses to accept the cat and sends it shooting back into the air, time and again, in dif- ferent twists and contortions. Even when it finally reaches solid ground, it doesn't stop, the sticky tarmac burning deep into the pads of its paws. Rustling in the maize, an occasional shaking among the stalks, reveal the course of its retreat to the farm.

II

The cleaner, Sonja, Anita, Jenny, always arrives five to ten minutes late. Five minutes before the agreed time, his levels of irritation start to rise. She never comes five minutes earlier to make up for all the times she's late. It's become normal, as if T has agreed to it after she discussed it with him. The front door always ajar, never having to ring the doorbell, perhaps she's come to think that's normal now as well; what could he have better to do than wait for her to arrive?

Subtle hints are lost on Sonja.

Nothing about her is quiet.

She has a rough voice. Not mean and hoarse from tobacco, just naturally unpolished and harsh. You have to see her face before you can believe a woman could produce a sound like that, that it's even possible for such a sound to come from a woman. A sound with just one volume setting, for all purposes. Although it's a physical characteristic, an entirely genetic matter, T doesn't believe it causes Sonja any actual suffering: she doesn't notice she speaks louder than just about anyone else. Or perhaps it just suits her that way.

*

It's never really come up for discussion. They have enough money, his wife knows they have enough money, that she certainly doesn't have to go out to work every day for the cash. T didn't push her in that direction; he wouldn't mind if the situation were different, but maybe it's better this way. He suspects she does it mainly for him, to give him the empty house during the daytime, his own exclusive company. Perhaps she wants some distance. She wants both of them still to be able to wonder what the other one is doing now. She wants to create an opportunity for them to miss each other, and to return home in the evening.

Is that why she makes herself so attractive? Is that why she takes her time in the bathroom in the morning? Does she want him, when he looks up from the newspaper, to think about other people looking at her desirable backside in those elegant black trousers? Does she want him to take pleasure in her, in the thought that she would allow only him, in the office toilet, to place his hands on her waist and press that bare whiteness against his pelvis? Does she too take pleasure, legs apart in that same toilet, in the effect she has on him?

Why should he play the starring role in her thoughts? She does it for herself, of course. To escape from him. She tells no-one at work who her husband is. To protect him, yes, that too, but mainly because she doesn't want to be associated with him. She wants a life of her own. She relishes the ordinary world of traffic jams, colleagues and targets. But how does that fit with the many irritations she brings home with her on a daily basis? Is she entangled in an invisible web of emancipatory masochism?

They each have their own bank account in addition to the joint one. Because it doesn't matter, he doesn't know how much she earns – *if* she earns anything. He can vaguely recall a novel about a businessman who, for many years, kisses his wife goodbye in the morning, leaves the house, but never arrives at an office. Does she, so as to give him a calm space to work in, so as not to saddle him with responsibility and guilt, for the sake of convenience and peace, sit reading all day long in a motorway service station? Does she have a pair of boots stashed somewhere and does she walk away the hours in the woods, in her black trousers? Or does some wild young artist, a painter without brushes, show her all the ins and outs of his studio? While she's cooking for her daughter and her husband, can she still feel him as she secretly clenches her buttocks?

He doesn't think so. That would make her not only an excellent writer but also an amazing actress: inventing all those little intrigues among colleagues, faking so many niggling irritations. His wife works in human resources. What would she do at home all day? Clean?

T objects to her always arriving late. He complains to his wife about the half-finished work, about the fixed route that Sonja/Anita/Jenny takes through the house without ever deviating, even if the dust bunnies are leaping up into her face. He loathes the frantic ringtone on her mobile phone. But most of all he dreads the "chat" every week, when the cleaning's over and the form has to be filled in, stamped. The chat is preceded by a shrill announcement from the foot of the stairs that she's finished, always ten minutes before the agreed time, and he answers her in his office, in a whisper, "No, you're not." Downstairs she fusses about with her handbag and shoes and car keys. She talks as if T is privy to her secrets, as if he's long known all the people she names so casually, as well as the relationships between them, and all the details of the events that she mentions in passing, because he, along with the rest of the world, knows what it's all about and everything that's gone before. It's the brazen assumption that leaves him speechless, the ease with which, in the presence of strangers, she remains the centre of the universe, articulating with confidence, a woman of sophistication. T can almost see the overmodulated waveforms emanating from her sandpapery larynx, hears them hitting the walls and bouncing off, transforming the living room into the acoustic equivalent of a wildly splashing aquarium. He clings to his rubber dinghy – a pen, a letter, a magazine – and waits out the storm with a smile on his face. He doesn't really know why. He settles on politeness. Or is he concerned about the picture this woman, a privileged witness, will paint of him in the village if the celebrity's not willing to have a little chat with the cleaning lady?

T hears the ding-dong deep in the house. While he waits, he looks back at the other side of the road. This is what Lodewijk and his wife see when they look at his house. What would he himself think, what kind of people would he imagine living in a house like his?

They immediately invite him in, warmly, as if this is a visit that was planned long ago, one they've been looking forward to. All that's missing is the china on the neatly laid table. They halt in the empty space between living room and front room when he brings up the reason for his visit: the blue basket. The basket Lodewijk used to collect the post when they were on holiday.

Lodewijk looks at his wife, briefly bows his head; yes, now he remembers, the blue basket, and to his wife he says: the coupon basket. It's a basket they keep coupons in, oh, a piece of junk, used to be her mother's, he thinks, coupons or an interesting newspaper article, a recipe; Lodewijk points at an armchair in the corner.

In his mind, T flicks on the reading lamp, sees the glasses on the tip of Lodewijk's nose, hears the whining request for the scissors, the good ones, directed at the kitchen, always at around half past five. His wife brings him the scissors, with slow steps, slight surliness, long arms hanging, but he ignores it. Anyway, he's doing it for her, isn't he?

T hears how Lodewijk says the word "junk". He's not the kind of man to surround himself with junk. They are pieces of junk, they have no value, but they have been selected by Lodewijk to become part of his ordered life and are therefore important, indispensable. The word "junk" is a confession, he knows what this is about, the memory is still strong. For a week, he turned his head away whenever he saw T in front of the house, an indication of silent rage, because T had not, in accordance with their explicit agreement, returned the blue basket before midday. T knew that he and his wife would be out in the afternoon, and wanted to leave punctually! Leaving the basket on the doorstep like rubbish, for the tomcats to spray.

A piece of junk.

Will the biographer who comes here to listen have a good enough ear to detect that obvious dissonance?

The biographer is sitting in the same chair where T is sitting now, he takes a biscuit and is surprised by the lace tablecloth. The atmosphere in the house reminds him of holidays at his grandparents' house. Warm memories. As he works a sliver of nut out of a tooth with his tongue, he can already picture the words "almond finger" in his book. He looks through the French windows, takes a mental snapshot of the garden. The fuss about the blue basket is intriguing. Why, several months after the event, did T go and apologise so profusely to Lodewijk and his wife? A year after his fatal accident, it's the first thing they think about.

Lodewijk still seems baffled, he repeats that he doesn't understand. What was it about? A blue basket, used to be her mother's, a piece of junk, look at it, here: junk. They're not people who would be that quick to take offence, are they? Is that how they seem? Like the sort of people who would immediately condemn others?

T and his daughter are standing between two fat conifers at the bottom of the garden. Before opening the rusty gate, he warns her to look left and right for any cyclists; Renée runs blindly onto the path.

It is the third day after the first time. The first time was a misunderstanding. He thought the woman at the end, or perhaps the beginning, of her long, narrow garden was looking at him. Laundry basket at her feet, hands on her hips. On an impulse, he raised his arm and waved. Perhaps she was looking at her dog by the rabbit hutch, about halfway between them, which he hadn't noticed from the path. Perhaps she'd realised the misunderstanding later that day. The man had waved at her as she looked in his direction, but she was actually keeping an eye on Filou. Or was it just a coincidence that she had another load of washing to hang up at the same time the next morning? And if not, if it had been a kind of apology for the previous day, then the third time, yesterday, must surely have been a coincidence. The coincidence of an irresistible spring breeze.

He sees no-one, he saunters, he thinks he can make out that the back door of the house isn't shut. He crouches, undoes his laces, ties them in a bow. He glances at his wristwatch; he estimates that he's about three minutes earlier than yesterday. He hears Renée shout, she's already reached the pavement, is waiting for him.

She's like a slender Ethiopian with a child too big to carry on her back, one edge of the full laundry basket resting on her hip bone, with her torso leaning in the other direction. At the washing line, she glances almost casually over the rabbit hutch, into the distance, sees him and waves with her free hand. T is standing again now, he waits for a couple of moments, as if allowing her greeting the time to cross that distance, and waves back, equally casually.

It doesn't mean anything. One day it will stop, maybe even tomorrow. They don't know each other. They wouldn't recognise each other in the queue at the baker's. There is no connection between them and they feel no need to approach each other. The image of her that exists within him, and of him within her, is therefore pure, untainted. All he sees is a slim woman hanging up the washing; all she sees is a father taking his little girl to school. Nothing more than that.

12

The itch had started as he was drying himself. Steegman knew for sure that he hadn't got any shampoo in his eyes. The explanation he always came up with was that the heat of the water had caused some reaction. He didn't have much faith in it; the itch was too deep, behind his left eye. Sometimes he tried turning the eyeball as far as he could, stretching the muscle and feeling, if only for the first few seconds, a pleasure like pressing a fingernail into a mosquito bite. Discomfort soon followed, though, and a sharp increase in the frequency of the flickering.

He took the ticket from the machine beside the barrier and drove into the underground car park.

How many of these small, vague complaints must doctors hear about every day? Too vague to prescribe a treatment. They shrug their shoulders, give it another prod, look more closely, mumble some medical jargon and finally advise the patient to wait and see. They point out the benefits of simple painkillers. For a general sense of wellbeing. Steegman had washed down two with a large snifter of Armagnac. He'd slipped his fountain pen into the inside pocket of his light-blue suit and called to Tereza that it really was time to go.

The flickering was making him dizzy. It was as if twice,

three times a second the light went off and flashed back on again. Every time, he had to refocus on his slightly altered surroundings; his vision was jerky, in slow motion, not flowing, not anticipating as it usually did. The approaching launch of his new novel was not going to pass before his eyes like a film but as a collection of images, disconnected frames.

On the way to the lift Tereza took his hand. In the long process from idea to publication this was the part he dreaded most: the walk from the parked car to the building where the writer of the brand-new book is expected. Going inside. The walk and then opening the door, the trapdoor.

Back above ground, he filled his lungs with the fresh breeze that swept across the square. When they still lived in the city, he often liked to visit this square, in the evening, at around this time of day. It was surrounded by banks, anonymous head offices that had restored the neo-classical facades to their former glory, none of them more than five storeys high. In one corner, the opera house stood almost shoulder to shoulder with a concert hall, with little room left for cafés and restaurants. The tourists, with their bellies and shorts, loitered in the shadow of the bell tower and the cathedral. But even when there were people, the wide open square appeared somehow deserted, in the middle of the city, with everyone reduced to their actual proportions.

Beside the tall glass doors of the concert-hall foyer, he recognised the cover of *The Murderer* on a smart display. A black background with identical emblematic heads of model citizens – red, yellow, blue – spying on one another out of the corners of their eyes. The designer's initial suggestion, right first time. His publisher liked it too, but pointed out that an actual design like this, rather than a photograph with lettering, wouldn't receive much enthusiasm from the bookshops. After a few email exchanges, they'd decided to keep the design; after all, Steegman had nothing to lose as yet. And, besides, you never knew. Perhaps the unconventional cover, the cheerful absurdity of the design, the suggestion of masterpieces from the 1950s might tempt more adventurous readers to buy the book. He should bear in mind that most writers like him found that kind of audience impossible to reach.

The design would not play any significant role this evening. His launches were always well attended and afterwards hailed as a great success: the high point in the brief life of his novels. The turnout wasn't a reflection of his popularity. He was lucky that Julie, Tereza's charming sister, ran the foyer and knew plenty of people, and that the evening was organised by a literature-loving bookseller with a thick address book. The result was his regular crowd of between 150 and 200, all keen to buy, and all of whom he should, by now, know by name.

The walk and going inside and having to angle for someone's name when writing an inscription in the book, the third introduction in a row.

He spotted his parents at the edge of the crowd. No-one would object if he said hello to his parents first. His mother's simplicity, her slightly faraway look when she entered unknown territory, calmed him; he turned his back on the noisy room and smiled right at her, a sign of affection, which she answered by briefly laying her hand on his cheek. I'm so proud of you, son. You know I'll never read your book, I can't concentrate, it's all too complicated for me, but I want you to know that I'm very proud of you and that I wish you all the happiness in the world. That gesture said it all at once. She was obviously delighted. She was happy that, so early in the evening, she'd had the opportunity, that her rather distant son had magnanimously given her that opportunity. The party was a success. She wouldn't mind leaving now. Get home nice and early.

Tereza was speaking to his father, who gave his son a kiss and then turned his mask of seriousness back to Tereza. Steegman didn't join in with the conversation. Soon he had a gin and tonic in his hand and he'd left the periphery; for the rest of the evening he would be unable to count on Tereza. He immersed himself in the bustling warmth of the group. Surrendered himself. He heard what he was saying, instantly found his stride. He listened to the lavishly lipsticked, fleshy mouth of a woman with jet-black hair, who looked as if she'd walked straight out of a silent movie, with her perfectly straight fringe – he expected to see a cigarette in a mother-of-pearl holder between her white gloved fingers. A former neighbour who'd undergone a metamorphosis. Who'd been single for so long that she'd come to present it as a virtue. He discovered, remembered from previous occasions, that as soon as he showed any willingness to speak, he didn't have to say much more. His unprompted surrender helped the guests to overcome a barrier. Their hesitation to be themselves on his evening, in the company of this celebrated author, melted away like snow in the sun.

He listened to the man who had gently pressured him to join his circle – one hand on his upper arm, his first name, twice. A man in his fifties, classic suit, gold tiepin, someone from the board, invited by Julie. He introduced his wife, his two teenage sons, Juul and Siel, awkward at hearing their own names. The Lottery, co-owners of the concert hall, a former guildhall, renovation, millions, the high ceiling, the columns, the pediments. Dates and years. Napoleon.

It was something Steegman hadn't seen for a long time, always men, with a slimy thread of old saliva between top and bottom lip, which keeps on snapping, then piling up in a disgusting lump on the moist base until the next b, p or m brings the lips together again. He stared at it, pointedly, wiped his own lips, but failed to influence the man. Couldn't he feel it himself? Didn't he know from experience? How many times must his wife have cleaned her own lips to draw his attention, indirectly, discreetly, to that revolting blob? How did he explain the obvious disgust on Juul and Siel's faces at the breakfast table?

It wouldn't be long now before the confession came, unashamedly, a little proudly: he did not read novels. He didn't have the time, but his wife read herself silly, locked herself away in the bedroom, as many as three books a week! Steegman didn't need to ask, the wife didn't need to say; he didn't want to hear it: thrillers.

Dozens of acquaintances within his field of vision. A nod here, a signal there, be with you in a minute. Where was the professor who was going to introduce his book, where was the PR woman from the publishing house, where was his editor? He didn't dare to stick his head up above the crowd. It seemed as if he could hear the rapid flickering of his eyelids, not on the outside, but through the inside, tiny waves within the aqueous humour. It was like the tapping hammers of his typewriter, it set him apart. At one time he had been hypersensitive to the tiny background noises of his computer, to all the sounds he heard when writing, but now he hid himself inside an impenetrable cocoon of clacking. The sound of his book drowned out the world.

In the blackness of the missing frames, he caught flashes of T. He attends the launch of his new novel incognito. Everyone there knows him, of course, but most of them from a photograph that's nine years old. A beard, shorter hair, or longer; different glasses, trainers, a T-shirt, and particularly the fact that no-one expects T to be at his own book launch – it all combines to make him completely invisible, a fly on the wall. This is an exclusive event. All the people the biographer will approach first are gathered here. He strolls past the small groups, listening, observing, noting how they've aged but not changed. Some of them he'd forgotten.

Steegman would have to leave T's parents at home. They would recognise him, give him away. His sister, Marie, and her beanpole of a boyfriend aren't there either. They belonged in a separate chapter. A family celebration. Not just anything, an important birthday, his father, his sixty-fifth. They don't go to a restaurant, his mother wants to have a cosy celebration at home, children, grandchildren. She's looking forward to organising the party, ordering lamb, flowers for the table, buying new linen. She takes the canteen of cutlery that she received as a wedding present out of the dresser, places it ready at the foot of the big clock. She locks herself away in the kitchen for two days, a Virginia Woolf-like passage, the simultaneous nature of events in her world, the memories that come steaming up, the ecstasy. That's as far as the comparison with Mrs Dalloway goes. She grew up surrounded by pigs, chickens and seven small children, whose mother she became at the age of twelve. When she was fourteen, she passed the torch to her sister and went out to work as a maid for a nouveau-riche family in the provincial capital. The closest she came to sophistication or the fine arts was on Friday mornings, when she dusted four Chinese vases on the landings of the central staircase, the porcelain so fine, she tells her son, that you could see the sun shining through it. Once she was married, she went to work with her husband at the factory. A furniture factory, say, home every day at quarter past four, the spicy scent of wood shavings, of mountains of white sawdust in his father's green overalls, varnish on his mother's apron, the crust of the fresh bread, the bottle of tangy beer always in the same spot on the windowsill, the cherry-red sparkle, as his father leafs through the paper at the kitchen counter, picking the dust out of his nose. The splash of the first peeled potato coincided exactly with the chink of the glasses, as he clinked with his good friend Barry, who was congratulating him again on *The Murderer*.

Along with Tereza and the editor they both shared, Barry was one of the trio to whom Steegman first gave his work to read. He was very well read and had the precision and rapid eloquence that work well on radio and T.V. His essays in the newspaper, in the literary supplements, also showed an enviable clarity and passion, and Steegman had been pleased to hear that, in Barry's opinion, any bad review of *The Murderer* could only signify ill-will on the part of the reviewer.

Although he hadn't doubted his friend's sincerity when Barry uttered this opinion between two puffs of his fat Cohiba, he couldn't help thinking of a passage in a novel, in which, following a pleasant visit from two close friends, a couple, or was it a party with a bunch of friends, that was also possible, the protagonist, who's the host, waits with the intercom phone up to his ear for the couple to step out of the lift and walk towards the loudspeaker, as he wants to tell them they've forgotten something upstairs, but the couple he hears must be different people, the tone of their conversation is serious, and then he recognises their voices, hears his own name and his wife's, drenched in venomous contempt.

Just as Steegman was attempting to capture his friend's appearance in a few striking images, notes for later, he asked him, ironically enough, if he was already working on a new book. Steegman always thought the word "book" sounded like a thick tome slamming shut, and something inside him slammed shut too, as he suddenly collided with the immense volume of his new book, of the book that had to be written over the next couple of years. An animated cartoon, something in 3D, he couldn't remember when, one of those incredibly expensive B.B.C. documentaries, demonstrating the events in the womb at the time of conception, and afterwards, the solitude of the brave sperm cell, that little pinhead with its quivering tail in a terrifying underworld, a microscopic universe, an odyssey full of dangers and enemies, with that huge bulwark gradually looming, the attraction, the thick, irregular wall through which the sperm desperately tries to worm its way.

His gaze fell on Barry's girlfriend, her prettiness, she said something to him, he nodded, didn't hear her, her deep-red hair sending him straight back into the book, *bisque de homard*, the starter, T spoons it up, *bisque de homard*, so rich and thick, almost brown, his mother's *pièce de résistance*, learned when she was a maid, when she had to do the dirty jobs in the kitchen, the fat cook lazy, but quick with her fists, the early highlight of the feast, the lamb undercooked, the cake too crumbly, the never-ending self-recrimination. After the starter, there's a little time, they have all afternoon, the children in bed, he slips out of the house. The streets have become narrower, the neighbourhood has shrunk, the sky is vast. So many people who just went on with their lives when he disappeared long ago, still close to one another and their relatives, to people like them, in their shared dialect, like living in a reservation; less than a forty-minute drive from his home, to be visited whenever he wanted. They have never been to Isfahan, never lived in Alexandria, never seen the Desert of the Tartars, travelled the Silk Road or drunk kir royal on the Orient Express, no, they're not characters in that kind of novel. But they have all known T, the strange blond boy, his father's son, the apple of his mother's eye, banished at an early young age to his imagination, distanced.

At the side of the small podium, by the bookshop's stand, he found Dominique, the P.R. lady. She'd lost at least fifteen kilos since he'd last seen her, at the presentation

89

of Barry's performance poems. Steegman didn't know whether to be concerned and enquire about her health or to compliment her on her diet. They held each other by the shoulders and, Dominique taking the lead, kissed three times. She gave him resounding, celebratory kisses. Or were they the more heartfelt kisses of an unspoken farewell? Or perhaps consolation, moral support, as the first thing she said was that there had been no requests for interviews. That was sure to change over the course of the week. She seemed to be implying that, if needed, she would rustle up an interview for him, that she'd deploy all of her charms on his behalf. She was wearing a delicious perfume, she had new glasses and a new, short outfit. Maybe the illness had unleashed an unbridled sense of vitality in her, perhaps that was how people became cured of the incurable. Maybe the illness had given her the figure she'd wanted all her adult life, and in the time remaining to her she would play all of the trump cards she'd been given, leaving not one fortunate side-effect of her sorry condition unexploited. Cheating on death by flirting whenever and wherever and with whomever she could.

Steegman said he didn't feel like doing interviews this time. He'd let the book speak for itself, he had nothing to add. But Dominique turned a deaf ear, she couldn't take that seriously from an author, she'd been in the business for twenty years. She came and stood beside him, as if to demonstrate that they belonged in the same camp, keep calm, it'll all turn out fine. Comrades in the battle for media attention.

They looked at the crowd. She said the turnout was

better than she'd expected. She said the professor was very enthusiastic about the book, she was expecting him at any moment, she'd just spoken to him on the phone, he was parking. Steegman felt her hand glide over the small of his back; she asked if he wanted another drink. The distinct impression that he could have asked for much more. Then the bookseller came over to say hello, to congratulate him. He took *The Murderer* from the table and looked at the book as if he were setting eyes on it for the first time. He read part of the blurb, flicked through the pages with his thumb and brought the author's photograph closer to his face. He asked if Steegman had had any say in the cover design, how it worked these days. Very smart, was his final conclusion: the book looked very smart. He gave the impression he was saying it because he really meant it. After Dominique's resounding kisses, the second consolation prize of the evening.

Steegman raised the glass to his mouth, but drank hardly any of the gin and tonic, enjoyed the ice against his top lip. Most probably Dominique, the bookseller was unlikely, the professor a definite – supporting characters with a part to play at T's book launch. He would have to mention Dominique's calves. He shared Barry's opinion that the female calf was underappreciated. The calf and, as far as Steegman was concerned, the instep of the foot, stretched inside an Italian summer sandal. The casual way some women at pavement cafés would lightly run two lacquered nails, ring and middle finger, over the taut instep of the dangling foot, one shoulder down, collarbone in the shade of a crisp, white blouse, neck at its longest, while still talking to the other side of the table.

For effect he would make Dominique a little younger, younger than forty, maybe give her darker skin, a Cuban grandfather. "Michèle" had a nice ring to it. The professor, though, in every respect, lived up to the visual connotations evoked by his title. Even as the man entered the room, some distance away from him, Steegman noticed that his head was in constant motion, nervous twitches on a thin neck, which at first he had blamed on his own visual tic, but which upon closer inspection was emphasised by the quivering tips of his greying hair. The professor had lots of hair, his face was surrounded by it, long and frizzy on top, wide, thin and stringy below – more pubic hair than beard. He was wearing a baggy black suit and a baggy white shirt. Logic and philosophy of science. A girlish giggle and a regional accent would soon win him the audience's approval.

The bookseller had first welcomed everyone to this very special occasion. In weighty tones, he had assigned Steegman a position among the greatest contemporary authors. That's right, the audience had heard that correctly – he held up his index finger: he had not specified a particular language. He paused for a moment, an opportunity for spontaneous applause, which was not forthcoming. Briefly he sketched the literary trajectory Steegman had followed thus far. Nearly all the promotional quotes he fired at the room came from insignificant publications, from "discussions" that included half of the blurb from the book. But his speech was well constructed, cogent, he'd worked hard on it, and – after all, this evening was Steegman's party – the praise was sincere. Then he announced what was to come, and introduced the professor, who, with a small bow, had just shaken Steegman's hand at the side of the podium – "the author".

The professor had read *The Murderer* with increasing astonishment and fascination. He described the protagonist, Ferdinand; that was the best place to start. Ferdinand is a man of seventy-three, a widower, who can no longer keep up with the rapidly changing times. He's becoming an outsider, and he knows it; he retreats to his terraced house just outside the historic centre of the town. He lives surrounded by waste paper, that's how the few people who still visit his house refer to his extensive library, as waste paper; the story's set in the future, but the professor was afraid this future was not all that distant. He cited the example of the calf-leather shoes, Ferdinand's moccasins, which nowadays have become prohibitively expensive. "Nowadays", the author wrote, almost casually, as if it were just a detail, the professor gave Steegman a meaningful look, "nowadays" meat for consumption is grown in huge factory laboratories. No animal feed filling up the fields, so there's more land to build on, no carbon dioxide emissions, and so more room for cars, no surplus of manure, no slaughterhouse waste, no disease in the food chain, and more meat, cheaper meat, for everyone. But also: no leather, an incidental side-effect. The elimination of animal cruelty, not the government's prime concern, is cleverly exploited in large advertising campaigns designed to quell the protests and complaints, featuring old photographs and video footage originally produced by the enemy camp. And here we came to the very heart of the book: the moral dilemmas associated with our attempt to find solutions to the problem of increasing overpopulation.

Steegman looked at the faces in the front row, hanging on the professor's every word. Was that the heart of his novel? He'd never seen it that way. For him, it had all been about Ferdinand. The rest was, as it were, a mental backdrop, brilliant clouds against a blue sky above a Descent from the Cross. But – who was it who had said this? – a book was always smarter than its writer. He filled his mouth with sparkling bitter-sourness. No, not that: a book was as smart as its reader. A good book, that is. Or had he said it himself?

A broad smile on his face, the professor argued that Steegman, in *The Murderer*, had put forward a solution that was particularly ingenious from a literary point of view. Soon he would have to tell him how he'd come up with his insane "Measure", a plan introduced by a cynical government, smuggled in under the pretext of avoiding the immorality of mandatory family planning. He shook his head; it was so absurd, so world-shaking, that after a few pages it had started to seem terrifyingly plausible. People sometimes said great writers were visionaries, didn't they? Well, here you have it. He held up the book and pointed at the cover. Did they see those little guys, those little faces, the way they were watching one another? Yesterday evening he'd been studying the design, and he'd drawn a few lines. He couldn't believe, as a professor of logic, that it was a coincidence that each of those heads was watched by the exact same number of other heads. They were locked in a visual clinch – it was impossible to imagine a better cover for this book. But to get back to the point. He stopped to ponder his words for a moment. He wanted to ask the audience a question. Imagine – and on this festive occasion he wanted to stress that this was only imaginary, it was not a licence – imagine they were allowed, permitted by law, by the authorities, to commit *one* murder, which person in this room would they choose to kill?

Chuckles, murmurs, hubbub.

His question had taken them by surprise – or maybe not! Perhaps they already had someone in mind, and had done for some time now, but they thought it wasn't worth the effort, or ultimately couldn't bring themselves to commit the deed. That wasn't a problem as such; after all, they weren't obliged to kill anyone. But, and here came the key question, he stroked his beard twice, how did they know for certain that no-one would murder *them*? In other words, wouldn't they almost feel forced to make use of their one permitted murder if they wanted to stay alive themselves? He drew a circle in the air, asked his question again: if it were allowed, whom would they murder right now?

Throughout the rest of his speech, he remained excited about the Measure, which, in *The Murderer*, involved not one murder, but two. He talked about the government's deceitful agenda. The Measure, with its chain reactions of impulsive revenge, would be used mainly in the lower social echelons, the most expensive when it comes to social security and medical care. Expenditure would fall dramatically, income taxes per capita would increase spectacularly. Security would prove self-regulating. The prediction was that in the first few years, when most murders would be committed, general levels of civility would increase exponentially, resulting in a morally superior society within only five years.

White clouds.

Barely a significant word about the fortunes of Ferdinand and his daughter.

After the professor, who received an appreciative round of applause, it was time for music, a cello suite by Bach, time for a little contemplation, presented by a music student whose shinbones curiously had the same curve as her bow.

The bookseller thanked her, "marvellous!", and also the professor for his enthusiasm. At the lunch and planning session a few months ago, he had insisted, yet again, that Steegman should go up onto the podium at the end and say a quick something; people expect it on this kind of evening, it wasn't over until that had happened. He'd welcomed them to the reception, generously supported by whoever it was, but not before giving the author the final word. Ladies and gentlemen, Emiel Steegman!

He held on to the edges of the metal lectern, leaned on his arms, raised his head. This position, he felt, happened to look nice and casual, particularly when the speaker had no paper in front of him. He could see everyone and no-one, and he listened as the words he'd memorised over the past week came flowing from his mouth. It would have seemed silly to read a speech of just three minutes from a sheet of paper, full of nothing but generalities, in a performance designed to make the audience believe the author was eloquently improvising; he was acting, playing the part of a Steegman who would never exist. At the bar behind the crowd, with its lounge lighting, he saw the staff silently filling glasses, between his words he heard rapid, brief glugging; young people, most likely students, in their first white shirts and black formal trousers, expertly instructed by Julie in how to pour the wine: not until the very last moment, half glasses – no-one likes white wine when it's warm. Tiptoeing, his editor joined the audience, delayed in the traffic, he'd come a long way, a polite man, not a man to arrive late. He folded his jacket over his arm and gave the author his full attention, without trying to make contact. Steegman could think of no obvious reason why the man might have designs on his life, or the other way around, but it was very likely that his own hypothetical murderer was in this room. The same group that would gather, one last time, in the sombre setting of a funeral parlour for his actual despatch. Since Renée's birth, Steegman had no longer entertained the popular fantasy of hovering over one's own coffin during the ceremony, as an all-seeing ghost. His pale, crying child hugged to the side of her dazed mother, that would spoil the pleasure of the daydream; he didn't want to be the cause of her grief. *Their* grief. The day before yesterday he'd made Renée stand in the corner, an attempt to put a stop to her obstinacy and theatrics, he'd sat in the same room, silently waiting for her to calm down and be quiet, and obediently turn her face to the wall, and when it was quiet, he'd looked at his watch, and thought: at least three minutes, more like five, he was her father, he had to bring her up properly, and then she saw Bear lying in the chair and the frantic crying began again, Bear, she wanted Bear, *her* Bear, he didn't know if she meant it or if she was just using Bear as a weapon in their showdown, and if she was really sad – yes, she was really sad – then could he "reward" her, in the middle of her punishment, by giving her Bear?

Wasn't that the wrong signal, something he would come to regret later? She kicked and cried until she ran out of breath, he sat silently gazing ahead, but actually looking at that limp rag of a toy, which was capable of undermining his authority, and then he shouted at her to be quiet, to stop blubbering, he yelled, he wanted to overwhelm her with his fury, not so much because of her behaviour at the dinner table, though that was the cause of this drama, but because her damn stubbornness was now forcing him to inflict this misery on her; he screamed out his love, but she didn't see it, she wasn't even four, what she would remember was the thunder and the silence, the silence of the man on the sofa behind her back, his incomprehensible cruelty. He could feel the flickering in his eyes increasing, as he thanked his typewriter for its sterling service, meant as a joke, a touch of levity, but this time with an undercurrent of emotion, the impression that he was fighting hard against his tears, he could see it on people's faces, on Marie's face, who seemed to be blinking along with her brother, the exhausting loneliness of writing, the superhuman exertion suddenly made palpable by a simple word of thanks to the noble instrument that had stood by him through every second of the trial, and which, perhaps as a result of this display of emotion, following his unexpected demise, tomorrow, next week, car accident, stroke, murder, would be buried with him, no doubt about it, it's what he would have wanted, Marie, in the austere room at the funeral home, the first reading, with this audience, all of whom will remember the thanks he gave at the book launch, a writer, a husband, a father, but also a brother, the main feature of her speech an anecdote she herself cannot recall, her near-death by drowning, a toddler in her grandparents' yard, the concrete cover of the well in the parched grass, her youngest uncle, sixteen, that winter he will die beside his Yamaha, throwing buckets of water with his strong arms, extinguishing the hot summer, teasing his six-year-old nephew – the swimming trunks, perhaps a word about the terry-towelling swimming trunks – and forgetting about his niece, she clings on tightly to the lectern, and she owes her life to her brother, a miracle, he hears something, feels something beneath the ground, her struggle, a muffled cry, a sixth sense and, just in time, he asks his playful uncle, that beautiful, budding man, where his sister has gone, and then he doesn't mention the incident for fifteen years because his uncle asked him not to, her brother, no-one can be silent more beautifully than her brother, she cries, before pulling herself together, and steering Tereza through that impossible day.

After his last word, he spotted her, Marie, applauding with her hands above her head, someone whistled through his teeth, the scrubbed students moved uncertainly through the crowd with their loaded trays; his novel was now no longer his, but theirs.

Dominique was waiting for Steegman at the foot of the stairs from the podium, a smile on her face. She kissed him, once, rubbed his back as if he were shivering with cold. She accompanied him to his chair at the table, where a woman was nervously taking her newly purchased book out of the plastic carrier bag. Start signing immediately, the bookseller had drummed into him, so people are quickly lured to the stand. Otherwise it would lose momentum and he wouldn't be able to shut up shop until after midnight. Steegman thought it was a good strategy, a practical arrangement, and – as long as he didn't stumble over the names – a pleasant duty, because, at the signing table, the line of people ensured conversation remained brief and superficial. Children, houses, jobs, a film, a trip, high-efficiency glazing. His relationship with many, with most, of these people, went no further than a chat while signing. They agreed to talk more, later, once the queue had cleared, a polite way to end a moribund conversation. As the host, he would see and speak to everyone, and the successful evening would be over in a flash.

It was no different this time. Shortly after eleven he slipped his fountain pen into his inside pocket and saw the stragglers gathered around a group of six tall tables that were laden with glasses. They seemed to be having a great time. Steegman stretched his legs and chatted to his editor, who'd been sitting beside him for a while, until a slap on his shoulder abruptly interrupted him; some drunk or other, he thought.

When he turned around, he was looking into the bright blue eyes of a rather stocky man. Flannel shirt, forest-green padded jacket. With an amused smile, he asked how Steegman was doing, the dialect came from the reservation. Facebook. As he said the word, he threw back his head, a kind of tic. He'd seen the book launch listed as an event on Facebook. Steegman accepted everyone as a friend, potential readers, every little helps. Jürgen, the man claimed he was Jürgen. Except for the eyes, there was nothing left of the boy he'd known, swallowed whole by time. A man and, what's more, a man who seemed old for his age. After a lengthy account of his messy divorce, he went on to installing solar panels. Once his small business had been reviewed, there was silence, and he asked rhetorically where the old days had gone, amused again, perhaps it was the drink after all. He had blunt teeth, pale gums. Steegman would never guess who he'd seen, a couple of weeks ago. Did Steegman know who he'd seen? He slapped him on the arm. "Sandra! I saw Sandra. In the Glass Street . . ." He took a step back and gave Steegman a big wink.

Was he still so childish, or had he come from so far, that even this euphemism for the local red-light district, widely used and not exactly discreet, was enough to make him wink? Or was he, by mentioning Sandra, all men together, bragging that he'd been visiting prostitutes? He didn't mean he'd seen Sandra in one of the windows, did he?

Sandra, a prostitute?

Steegman refused to respond to Jürgen's revelation, as if he didn't want to surrender Sandra's fate, not to this man. He made space for his editor to step between them, sensing that he was about to leave, it was a long drive. And in the boot of his car he had fifteen author's copies of *The Murderer*. As agreed, Steegman would walk with him.

13

T has a secret.

14

It was the first day of the summer holidays, it was grey, it was drizzling. Everyone would be staying indoors. Renée was watching "Cinderella". To the right of the brick shed, with the chicken coop on the left, Steegman found shelter from the wet, the breeze and the prying eyes. He made balls of paper, they burned just as well and didn't suddenly take off into the air.

T had shaken him awake the night before and whispered that he should leave nothing to chance. Making T do it, but sticking to the same old thing himself, that was tempting fate. Everything he was shielding T from, no matter how unlikely, could also happen to him. Besides, wasn't he the main character in a book based on Steegman's life, didn't he make love with his wife, didn't he look after his child? He'd rooted his idea in reality, and he mustn't forget to water it. A novel that was designed to expose our obsession with reality and true-life events, with the story behind the story, T had said, was something that couldn't simply be left to his imagination; it would have to be experienced in order to be believed.

At ten past four Steegman was sitting at his computer with a coffee. He carefully composed a casual-sounding email, which he sent to the people with whom he had regular contact, an urgent request to delete all of his old messages. He studied the settings of his Facebook page, he'd seen other people say goodbye, it was possible, a digital wheel clamp. Hadn't he read that there was a company that specialised in this, a cleaning service? As he clicked in the Google search bar, the endless trail of slime that he'd left across the internet over the years lit up within his mind; every address visited was recorded, every search term. A chain of D.N.A. that would allow an academic or some other bright spark to reconstruct his life. Day by day.

T doesn't have a computer. He reads the newspaper, watches television, he writes a letter. He has a landline, a phone with a dial, long before it came back into fashion. T does not want to be filmed. He is the only writer of his generation who has become world-famous without appearing on television; he's world-famous for that, too. The camera is objective, but it is operated by people. T is not a politician or an actor, he is not equipped to hold his own in this mutual manipulation of the image, and he refuses to allow his reputation as a writer in the public eye to depend on that process. It would be unfair. Anyone nowadays who still allows himself to be tempted, thinking it's an honour to be filmed, is seriously misguided. The flood of images has not taught us to watch more carefully but to judge more quickly. Smartphone video clips travel around the world at the speed of light, making people and breaking them. Big Brother has gone from tyrant to neoliberal, dearly paid in thousands of millions of trouser pockets.

Steegman placed a brick on the stack of paper, which

was about half a metre high, and went to fetch the folding chair from the garden shed. The longest, windowless wall had concrete shelves with dividers, cages for small pets, rabbits maybe, perhaps brooding pens for chickens, rather roomy ones. The bricks were crumbling in places, and where the reinforcing steel had been exposed to the damp, the rust was flaking. He'd always found it an eerie place, even before the wristband had turned up a week ago, when he was rummaging around for the shears in one of the high boxes. Faded orange plastic, a toy from a doctor's bag: the wristband had a label, but the ink on the strip of paper had vanished, all except for one vague vertical line of the first letter.

There was plenty of variation in the way people wrote a capital V. Tereza was certain the wristband didn't belong to Renée.

How did it end up so high and deep in the boxes if someone hadn't put it there on purpose? And what reason would anyone have for putting it up there? There were better ways to make it disappear. The intention must have been to hide it. But surely, if someone had gone missing, the police would have taken the trouble of fetching a ladder to search the highest shelves?

The ivy on the old bricks of the shed reminded him of that British crime series on Saturday evenings, set in and around a charming little village. There were two or three murders per episode, never scary, often ingenious, carried out by members of the upper middle class or respectable domestic staff, a tangle of relationships and motives, that was what it was all about. Had the family of bakers become ensnared within such a complicated web? Did one half of the village suspect what the other half was keeping silent about? And did François and Arlette belong to neither camp?

The ways of fate were strange, to say the least: an identification bracelet, here, of a child who had vanished without a trace.

As one ball of paper burned to a cinder in the decorative terracotta pot, he read parts of the next sheet. The chance that this would one day be worth something, a small inheritance for Renée, was zero. Endlessly rewritten paragraphs. Dozens of pages of nonsense, written to test a newly acquired typewriter, or simply for the sake of typing away without writing, for the pleasure – this in particular would be irresistible material, capable of proving any argument. People would hear the voice of his subconscious in it, summoned in some unguarded moment. Documents revealing his true face, as the Shroud of Turin shows the face of Jesus Christ.

15

"Daddy!" Renée threw her arms around his legs, he didn't have the chance to get inside. But, just for a moment, he'd seen the excitement on her face. He thought it was strange, how after two nights at Grandma's she seemed to have changed, an illusion, something about her hair, about the light. Grandma, his mother, stood beaming in the doorway at the end of the hall. She said she'd been good. Had she been good? Renée nodded without releasing her grip around his legs.

His entire childhood, and even when he was already an adult – as long as he'd lived here, this had always been his favourite moment of the week: just before midday on Saturday, the sunlight through the long kitchen window, the charts on the radio, his mother cutting the chips, washing the lettuce, crushing peppercorns onto the purple steak on the unfolded, checked paper. He sat with his daughter at the same table as then. They ate from the same plates with the same cutlery. He couldn't stop sneaking glances at her. She ate with the appetite and focus that only a child can. Moist lips, pursed mouth, tasting every mouthful. Homemade mayonnaise, yellow and firm.

A flat ride, his father said. Arrival in Toulouse, right up Cavendish's street. Steegman would like to stay and watch with his father; the languorous delight of a flat stage of the Tour. Whiling away the time. Nothing that needed to be done. Holiday snapshots and a mass sprint. But they had to be back by one thirty. Renée was expected at her friend Amélie's birthday party. Grandma still had to wrap the present: princess paper and a big bow with glitter. Then Renée wanted her hair in a ponytail.

Steegman didn't feel so great in the car. He'd eaten too much and had three beers. A group of five unknowns was riding eight minutes ahead of the peloton. He pictured the brightly coloured group moving in a block along a wide road. Renée sat up uncomfortably straight in her seat, she refused to lean back and nap, not with her ponytail. Soon she was dangling forwards, like a ragdoll. They were almost at the village, they were almost at Amélie's party, which Renée was so looking forward to, when she woke up and announced, proudly, happily, "Daddy, I went to sleep!" They were driving through a green and rolling landscape, Kylie Minogue's summer hit on the radio, with the chorus, "You got it! You're wa-wa-wa-wow!" Both of them sang along, Renée mimicking the sounds, they clapped their hands, danced in their seats, and smiled at each other in the rear-view mirror.

He takes good care of his bicycle. Without his bike, he's nothing, helpless as a cowboy without a horse. The distances around the neighbourhood aren't impossible without one, but the others all have bikes, so he'd always be left behind. He'd have to run after them, worrying that, once he'd reached the dismounted group, they'd suddenly get bored and decide to go in search of another spot and, with no way for him to stop them, they'd jump onto their bikes and disappear. Particularly humiliating for the oldest one in the gang. He doesn't have the strength to impose his will without a bike. No-one does. The bike reigns supreme, is always right. One puncture and the day is ruined. You have to hope for a backie on someone else's bike, but they don't wait for anyone, you need to keep ahead of the situation, jump on in time, and the agreement can be unilaterally broken at any moment. His grandpa gave him his bike at his confirmation, six speeds, cloud nine. Beheyt, Benoni Beheyt, the man was once world champion, now he runs a bike shop; his name is signed on the horizontal tube of the frame. But when they do sprints, he's Freddy Maertens. Halfway down the street he's caught up; at the finish line he throws his arms in the air. They sprint, they race against the clock (around the block), and they play "forcefield", where the trick is to keep your balance, to manoeuvre yourself into a position where you can force your opponent into the kerb and make them put their foot on the ground. Forcefield!

Eighteen kilometres from the finish line, Steegman woke with a start. The peloton was keeping the riders' lead to forty-five seconds, within reach, the race was under control. It was after four thirty, the time he was supposed to pick up Renée from the party. He was lying on the two-seater sofa with his feet dangling over the edge. The stage had been slower than expected, there had been a strong headwind. He knew Cavendish would win, everyone knew. He was waiting out of laziness. Now that he had the chance to see the arrival, he wanted to watch.

Mieke and Paul, Amélie's parents, lived at the other end of the street, the top end, on a bend. He decided to walk. Still a little light-headed after his sleep, he wasn't in the mood for conversation. He hoped Renée would come with him right away, without complaining, that the afternoon's programme was over, that he wouldn't have to endure a puppet show.

"She's asleep."

He looked at Mieke's face and waited on the doorstep. He didn't know her well enough to read her smile. Renée? Asleep at a birthday party?

"Yes, really. She's asleep."

"Seriously?"

"Only a quarter of an hour or so."

"Did she ask if she could have a nap?"

"Why don't you come on in?"

The family was gathered around the dining table in the front part of the house. Most of them had pushed their chairs back a little. The cake, all but one crumbling slice, had been eaten, glasses of dark-brown beer stood beside the men's coffee cups. He sometimes saw Mieke's parents at the school gate; they came over to say hello.

"She's asleep," said the woman, a question in her voice.

"So Mieke just said. She must have been tired. All the excitement, I suppose. It's strange, though."

"Does she still have an afternoon nap at home?"

"Not for over a year now. No more than a few winks. Just now in the car, on the way here, a quarter of an hour, twenty minutes, no longer than that. But a proper sleep in her bed in the afternoon – no, it must be a year ago now."

"Sleeping never hurt anyone, though, eh?" said the man.

The family and friends around the table agreed with him. When a child wanted to sleep, said another woman, possibly Paul's mother – he was a soldier on a mission abroad – when a child wanted to sleep, then it was tired. Simple.

"The more they sleep," someone joked, "the better."

It was strange, though, Steegman repeated, because she'd been looking forward to the party for so long. He couldn't remember it happening ever before, not when they'd visited friends or gone to a party. Not even with family. They couldn't get her into bed, not even if she was exhausted. No, his little madam was too grown-up for that.

"She's not in bed," said Mieke. "We put her down here, with us."

The living room was in the middle of the house, next to the kitchen. Mieke stood by the sofa, where Renée lay still beneath a thin blanket with Winnie-the-Pooh on it. It seemed so unlikely that she'd be asleep, here, in a room full of strangers. Perhaps she'd wanted some attention because she was feeling a little ignored; it was, after all, Amélie's party. A smile on his face, he walked over to her, she'd kept up her act even when he was in the same room and she could hear his voice, even when everyone began talking about her. He gently brushed the hair from her forehead. She kept her eyes shut. He said her name, close to her face, kissed her on the cheek, smelled sweets.

111

"They had a great time," said Mieke. "Dieter spent almost the entire afternoon with them."

None of the men present made himself known as Dieter. Only now did he hear children, outside, in the garden, just a couple. The kitchen had only a side window, next to the open door with the insect screen. Steegman said her name again and told her to wake up, they were going home, come on, sweetheart. He gently shook her shoulder.

"Twenty minutes ago," said Mieke. "She came inside and tugged on Dieter's arm, she said her right leg felt funny and then she started crying. But we couldn't see anything wrong with her leg. So I gave her a bit of a cuddle and tried to comfort her, and she went straight to sleep. It was already gone half four. I thought, Emiel's going to be here any minute, so I won't phone him. She was sleeping so peacefully."

Mieke and Steegman examined Renée's right leg. No cuts, no bruises. There was nothing to see.

"Come on, sweetheart. Wake up." He spoke in his normal voice. He shook her shoulder. "If you like, you can sleep some more in your bed at home."

He sat down on the edge of the orange sofa and hoisted her onto his lap, but she refused to sit up straight, and he felt her full weight. She frowned, made a groaning sound and looked like she was sleeping soundly again.

Amélie appeared in the kitchen, a gold crown on her head. The young man who was following her must be Dieter. They kept their distance from the scene. Amélie asked her mum if Renée was still asleep. Elise, Amélie's little sister, came in, too. Everyone watched as she skipped, humming, to the corner of the kitchen, to the

112

large brushed aluminium fridge. She took a pink carton with a pink straw from the fridge door. Her humming briefly paused as she swallowed.

Steegman laid his daughter on the sofa, covered her up. He remembered the night, recently, when he'd heard her talking. He'd hurried to her room, she was sitting up straight in bed and looking at him angrily. She said something about men in black suits, but she didn't respond to his questions. He'd felt as if he were asking the wrong questions and she was waiting for the right ones, looking at him as if she could barely tolerate him. Suddenly she'd collapsed and closed her eyes.

"When they're really sound asleep, it's hard to wake children up," said a bearded man at the table, turning to the woman beside him. She started talking about her neighbour's grandchild, about fireworks above their house on New Year's Eve, about one explosion that had blown the glass out of their dormer window and how the boy next door, Alexander, a year or two older than Renée, had slept all the way through it.

"Leave her for a bit," said Mieke's father.

"Give Emiel a cup of coffee," said her mother. "Milk and sugar?"

"Black's fine," said Steegman.

"Black," said her mother.

Dieter came over and sat down on the coffee table. He looked at Renée, his head on one side. He said she'd played all afternoon. He had a plain brown leather cord knotted around his neck, no pendant. In his twenties, a member of some youth or nature organisation. While some of the men around the table discussed Cavendish's sprint, Dieter said he hadn't noticed anything about her leg. She could feel something, she'd said, but it wasn't an itch and it wasn't a pain. She'd cried a bit and then fallen asleep in Mieke's arms.

Steegman followed Dieter's gaze as he looked at Renée. He stroked the side of her head. Was she just pretending? So why was she being so stubbornly persistent? Was this an expression of her indignation, a swipe at him? Was he her target? But she'd been playing happily all afternoon. Dieter had paid attention to her.

Mieke held a thick cup under the spout of a thermal jug in the centre of the dining table. She pressed the big button several times to pump out the last few drops of coffee. She carried the cup on an equally thick saucer over to Steegman's outstretched hand. She paused. Was the coffee still hot enough? Was he sure? It wouldn't be any trouble to make some more. He was sure. He put down the saucer next to Dieter on the coffee table. He wanted to go home.

Without saying anything, he lifted Renée onto his lap. There was a silence, he knew everyone at the table was watching. He hugged her to his chest, her legs strangely twisted beside him. She didn't put her arms around him. He had to support her head.

"Renée? Wake up!"

He patted her cheek.

She protested, a strange, almost animal-like sound coming from her throat. Face and mouth contorted, she tried to find a comfortable position. Tried to sleep.

"Come on," said Steegman firmly. "We're going home."

Renée slept. Between her eyebrows was a deep, disgruntled groove. On her eyelids, a pale-green sheen.

Something wasn't right.

He looked Mieke in the eyes and said, "This isn't normal." He was shocked at his own words, his seriousness, even more than Mieke was. He felt his face flushing. He didn't want to be a burden to this family at their party. But he could sense that Mieke, herself the mother of young children, felt exactly as he was feeling. She'd probably been feeling that way for a while, maybe even from the outset, but Renée had simply fallen asleep, and her dad would be there any minute.

Dieter silently stood up and walked away.

Mieke took Dieter's place, after helping Steegman to lay Renée down on the sofa again; his little girl was resting with her head on his left thigh now. He told the story about her angry nocturnal episode, he told it so that everyone at the table could hear it, too. It was all he could think of, that she'd slipped into a very deep sleep, just as she had before, and she'd soon wake up again.

"I think you're right," said the bearded man's wife. "It's all been too much for her, she just needs to switch everything off for a while."

"You can't stop a child who wants to sleep," said the man himself.

The conversations around the table picked up, intersecting, centring on the peculiarities of small children. They were sitting there, Mieke and Steegman here. It seemed as if, as far as the talkers were concerned, Renée had ceased to exist. They played with the dessert cutlery, had a swig of beer, told stories in the same tone they'd have used even without Renée. A queasy, empty feeling took hold of his guts. The taste of the weak coffee tainted his mouth. He tried to swallow it away, he wanted to think. She didn't have a temperature. She was breathing. She was asleep. In a strange room, among strange people, in the afternoon. He looked at Mieke. She responded: "Do you want me to call a doctor? Shall I call the doctor?"

Another silence.

Why wouldn't Renée wake up?

He left the sofa, put his hands under his daughter's armpits and lifted her up. He repeated her name, a command, tried to make her stand. The only result was a new expression on her face, as if she were pondering a tricky problem and, eyes tightly shut, did not want to be disturbed.

"Call Mark," said Mieke's mother. "You've got his mobile number, haven't you? He'll come right away. Mark comes out for all of us," she said to Steegman. "I don't think he's on duty this weekend, but if Mieke calls him, he'll be here right away. – Just call him. Mark won't mind."

"That might not be necessary," said Steegman. "I'm sure she'll start to wake up soon."

He hugged her to his chest. He apologised. This had never happened before, except for that one time, that night. She just had to break out of her trance. That was all. She can't hear us.

Mieke went out into the garden to call the doctor.

Steegman held his daughter, almost four years old, in his arms like a baby. He was sitting on an orange sofa, beside the far armrest. The orange of the armchair was no longer the same orange as the three-seater sofa. Thick, rough, hard-wearing fabric. On the chimney breast of the bricked-up fireplace hung a collection of pale wooden frames, photographs and reproductions; at the centre of this jumble he recognised the colours and the calm of Edward Hopper. He wanted to be the woman in the train compartment, done up to the nines, hidden beneath a hat, engrossed in a book. Alone. Alone with Renée, away from the people around the table, who hesitantly began to talk about her, in muted tones, how happily she'd been playing, then come in laughing, how she'd skipped around Dieter. She hadn't even been crying for a minute when she fell asleep. One of them had thought to himself: what a happy little girl.

"I've spoken to Mark," said Mieke, slightly out of breath. "He's coming right now. No more than ten minutes."

Relief around the table. Mark was on his way. Steegman tried to share their relief. He concentrated on Renée's face. He leaned towards her and whispered that a doctor was coming, but that she could still open her eyes now, and they'd just go home. Daddy wouldn't be angry. He promised. And a promise was a promise.

After a while Mieke's mother came to sit beside him. She put a hand on Renée's knee and leaned over to look at the little girl. "He lives just outside the village," she said. "We can call him any time. It won't be long now."

Just as she was struggling up from the sofa, the door-bell rang. She raised one finger. Someone at the table responded with the same gesture.

Mark was wearing casuals: a striped polo shirt and a pale pair of jeans. He was one of those fifty-something authority figures who benefit from their dark weekday suits in so many ways. He entered with a vague greeting to everyone, but didn't deem Steegman worthy of a glance. Grouchily, perhaps because of the phone call, he said, "So what do we have here?" He looked at Mieke. "What exactly happened?" He put down his sharp-edged case on the rug next to Steegman's feet; the case, the polo shirt, the jeans: a knife pedlar from the former Eastern Bloc.

Mieke gave her account of the afternoon, thinking carefully to make sure she didn't forget anything. As she spoke, the doctor listened to Renée's heart. He checked her blood pressure, lifted her eyelids and shone a light into her pupils. He examined her leg. He looked through her hair for signs of a head injury.

Steegman told him about that one night, the trance.

Then everything fell silent.

The doctor kneeled beside his open case and looked at Renée, along with everyone else in the room.

"And you can't get . . ."

"Renée," said Steegman.

"Renée. You can't get Renée to wake up?"

"She did groan, though," said Mieke's mother.

"She hasn't opened her eyes yet," said Steegman.

The doctor slapped her on the cheek, three times, quickly, and called her name in her ear. Then he asked Steegman to stand her up on the rug. She collapsed. The sound she made in her throat was pitiful. She scrambled up for her father's warmth and disappeared back into the depths.

"Well, I can't see anything," said the doctor. "Just let her sleep it off. She obviously wants to sleep. You could have an E.E.G. done at the hospital sometime next week,

118

perhaps something will show up. I don't think there's much to worry about."

"But she won't wake up," said Steegman.

"Oh, but she was awake, just now." He closed his case. "She's tired."

"She never sleeps in the afternoon. Not anymore."

"Well, she's asleep now, isn't she? Now she's too tired not to sleep. The E.E.G. will show us if there's a problem. I can't look inside her head. Get your doctor to make an appointment on Monday morning. That seems like the best course of action."

The doctor filled in the form for the health insurance, tore it from the block of carbon paper and put it on the coffee table. Before Steegman could say he didn't have any money with him, Mieke had rushed for her purse and paid Mark. Her parents walked with them into the hallway, thanking him profusely for coming out on a Saturday.

Around the table, the guests waited for the return of the three people who had brought the rest of them together this afternoon.

Renée was lying across his legs, her head resting on his right arm. With his free hand, he dug his mobile phone out of his pocket. He decided to send a text message; if he spoke to Tereza, he'd have to explain everything. She might misunderstand what he was saying and panic and crash into someone. By now she must be near the village anyway, back from the city, from her mother's. He wrote that she should come to Mieke's, that he and Renée were still there. He immediately received a kiss as confirmation, just an x, she had no time to type anything more. She was on her way.

"It's the electricity," said Mieke's mother, when everyone was gathered again. "Those scans measure the activity of the brain. It's electricity, Mark says. It can tell the doctors a lot."

Mieke asked if anyone wanted a drink.

No-one did.

"When you're asleep, there's less electricity."

Steegman said that he had let Tereza know. Without telling her anything. In the long silence that followed, apparently caused by the mention of Renée's mother, sounds floated through from the garden, great excitement from Amélie and Elise; Steegman imagined Dieter lying on the ground, with the girls besieging him. He pictured the three of them, Tereza, Renée and himself, leaving this house, laughing. He would take Tereza's car and watch their daughter skipping down the street, holding her mother's hand. He would wait for them in front of the house, and Renée – in spite of his warnings – would come running from a distance, too fast, her arms open wide: "Daddy!" She would have woken up when she heard her mother's voice. Mieke would have poured dark-brown beer. The older guests would have talked to one another about whatever they normally talked about and she would have spoken to Mieke about the school holidays, about travel plans, about the girls, who were still out playing in the garden. The day would simply slot itself back in among all the other days.

He looked at her closed eyes, stroked her forehead.

The doctor had called.

A doctor had examined her. She was asleep.

According to the doctor, she'd been awake.

Everyone stayed calm.

They were older people, they had experience.

It's hard to wake up a child who's really fast asleep.

Two cars came down the road, close together, as if one were towing the other.

A gang of squabbling sparrows skimmed past the big window. Then the deep cooing of a turtle-dove started up somewhere nearby; he remembered the nest in the angle of the drainpipe at the front of the house. Summer. Outside, it was summer.

The sound of a car slowing down.

The bearded man's wife stood up and asked if Tereza drove a black car.

"Dark," said Steegman. "Anthracite. A Ford."

"Is that a Ford?" She tapped her husband hard on the back of the head.

Could be. Could be a Ford, the man said.

Mieke went to look through the window. It was the neighbour's brother. Filip. It was a Volkswagen, a Golf.

"She drives a Ford," said Mieke's mother.

"It's Filip," said Mieke.

They heard the neighbour's doorbell. Filip's deep voice, his conversation in the hallway with his sister. It sounded abrupt.

The voices disappeared into the house.

The longer he looked at her, the more it seemed that the woman in the train compartment was not reading her book. She was pretending, so she could look away from the living room. She was hiding behind her hat because she couldn't bear to watch: Steegman pinned to an orange sofa by the stares of strangers, Renée on his lap, like a book, a wonderful book in a language he suddenly didn't understand.

If you lose, suggests Jürgen, the winner gets to kiss you. He immediately goes after Petra. Both girls protest, but they ride their bikes, they join in the game. After just a couple of minutes Jürgen comes to help the other boys to force Sandra to put her foot on the ground; Petra's too good. Sandra keeps on smiling demurely as she's surrounded, she fixes her eyes on the black tarmac, the tyre of her front wheel is pressed flat as she swerves. Before she's forced, she calmly gets off, props her bike on the kickstand and wanders into the grass. The boys, momentarily confused, shout after her that giving up is the same as losing. Petra yells something, Sandra doesn't look back, but starts running.

It's not the first time they've played a game with a kiss as the stake; the girls hold their lips together and submit, and that's it. Sandra lies down, sprawls in the long grass, Jürgen and Andy kneel beside her. He's standing at her feet, hands on his hips. They're panting, it's so hot. She says she'll only allow one kiss, they'll have to decide who's won. Jürgen and Andy giggle like girls and both look at him.

Maybe it's the change in her bikini, the way she shifts its contents, suddenly crossing her arms, making the sagging redness swell, how she primly closes that one open leg, the pale skin high on the inside of her thigh. Maybe the grass, which has swallowed her up, or the soporific hum of the insects. Maybe his impression, for the first time, that he may have been mistaken, that her big, dark eyes are not artfully penetrating the mysteries of life, but constantly anticipating it with a slight sense of panic.

A brief struggle, they soon have her under control.

On his instructions, Jürgen hooks one finger under the strap that's tied in a bow behind her neck in two big loops, on the side where the weight's leaning into the fabric. The breast slides smoothly out of the bikini, the sight of it almost makes Jürgen and Andy let go.

He says no clear instructions were specified regarding the kiss.

He names Andy as the winner.

Nervously, eyes moist, Andy finally presses his lips to the dark brown wrinkled skin rising stiffly from the breast.

Jürgen bursts out laughing and runs back to Petra, she's riding round in circles on the tarmac. Sandra's leg is free to kick out but it stays where it is; one leg isn't enough.

He notices that her eyes are dark mainly because of her dilated pupils. They take in everything, greedily, she doesn't want to miss anything. She doesn't object to falling into the boys' clutches, their superior strength, enduring it with a certain satisfaction.

Maybe she doesn't kick because it's over now, she doesn't expect anything more than the breast, the kiss. To him, it doesn't feel like they managed to capture her, not really, she saw this coming, she's secretly laughing at their fumbling, their childishness.

As he slides his hand into the leg of her baggy shorts, her expression changes. She squeezes her legs closed. After a fierce struggle, her face is flushed, hair clings to her forehead, she looks him straight in the eyes, must see his surprise when he exposes a thick bush of curly hair.

Andy doesn't understand his question.

Andy doesn't dare, he keeps his outstretched forefinger at a distance, as if anticipating an attack from a cornered rat.

He assures Andy that there's nothing to be afraid of. Andy tries, it doesn't work, takes some finding. Then his whole finger disappears into the coarse hair.

No-one moves.

No-one says a word.

A lark rises over Farmer Tuyt's sheep shed.

Andy's finger is inside Sandra.

One breast is hanging out of her bikini.

But she is looking at Emiel as if it is not she who is revealing intimate secrets; she looks as if she is seeing *him*. In the wide-open, gleaming blackness that regards him so intently, she reveals who he is. Not a leader, a chicken. Too cowardly to do himself what he always instructs others to do. He feels naked, he feels his mouth tense up in her gaze. As long as he is pinning her down, she has him in a headlock.

The moment she saw her, the colour drained from Tereza's face.

He'd heard her say hello, then Mieke briefly telling her what had happened. The word "doctor" had been mentioned.

She inched over to the fireplace opposite the sofa, kept her distance, didn't come any closer to him and Renée. She looked as if she'd seen a ghost. Her clothes, her keys hanging half out of her handbag, the sunglasses in her hair. She'd come from a different world.

"An ambulance," she said. "Now."

"Calm down," said Steegman. "A doctor came. He examined her."

"Why didn't you call an ambulance? She's pale. She never sleeps in the daytime!"

Steegman shouted that a doctor had been. He yelled out his frustration about that entire wretched afternoon.

Mieke, in the doorway, started crying.

Hands trembling, Tereza looked for her phone.

He stroked Renée's cheek. He said Mummy was there, asked her if she'd open her eyes now.

He heard Tereza in the kitchen, calm, polite, to the point, as if she knew exactly how things worked on the other end of the line, how, loudly and clearly, to convey the seriousness of the matter and how to elicit an equally efficient response.

Mieke dabbed her tears, she was only crying with her eyes, she was able to tell Tereza the story: the leg, the crying, the sleeping.

The paramedics arrived within just a few minutes.

There was confusion, the paramedics in their high-vis vests associated a "sleeping child" with a bedroom, they asked where the bedroom was, a bewildered Mieke showed them the way and they stormed upstairs, dragging two heavy bags of equipment, and so Steegman carried Renée upstairs because he thought the doctors wanted to examine her on a bed, in private.

In the tense silence, he made out the sirens of the ambulance, perhaps still a kilometre away. It was an ambulance for Renée, it was finding its way to this house, to this room; that idea bounced around inside his head. He imagined the streets the ambulance was driving along, didn't know if he should quickly come up with the shortest route or if he could still make it all go away by sending it in the wrong direction. Then the head medic said they'd take Renée to the hospital in Z.

Tereza asked them, half apologetically, please to take her to the university hospital in G., but the medic couldn't do that. He spoke softly, smoothly. Z. was a ten-minute drive away; G., the provincial capital, was more than half an hour. It was his responsibility, it was too dangerous, a long drive could cause any blood clots to move and result in further damage. They always had to drive to the nearest hospital first, that was standard procedure.

Blood clots? Had she had a stroke?

He couldn't answer that with any certainty. Two nurses, a fat one and a young one, manoeuvred their stretcher into the bedroom and looked at the head medic for instructions.

"We won't drive too quickly. We'll be really careful."

Downstairs, the visitors had gathered in silence on the front lawn. Mieke was crying even harder now and she quietly whispered sorry to Steegman. He put his arms around her and told her it wasn't her fault.

He waited in Tereza's car until the ambulance slowly passed him. The windows were frosted glass; he could see the fat nurse's shadow.

As they left the village and drove by vast, undulating fields of corn, his eyes filled with tears. He wanted to take her place. He was her father, what wouldn't he sacrifice, what wouldn't he promise to make everything alright again?

Don't pray, he thought angrily. Don't you dare pray.

He felt his phone vibrating. He undid his safety belt and stretched his leg, saw it wasn't Tereza with news from the ambulance, but his publisher, and decided not to answer, to keep the line free. Almost a minute later, the signal came to say he had a voicemail.

The A. & E. department in the basement of the building was practically deserted. A Saturday in the summer holidays in a small town. A paediatrician, a stern-looking middle-aged woman, was waiting for them. She said the radiologist would be along any minute. The curtains around the bed were half closed, everything was immaculate, Steegman could smell his own sweat.

The C.T. scan did not reveal a blood clot.

The doctor said blood clots hardly ever occur in children. The C.T. scan hadn't picked up anything in the brain. No, no clot. Tereza squeezed his hand hard.

The E.E.G. was tricky. The electrodes wouldn't stick properly. The radiologist saw a strange pattern on the printout. Then he said he had to consult with the doctor.

The wait was twenty-three minutes. Just as the paediatrician gave the curtain a tug, Renée opened her eyes. She reached for Tereza. The sounds in her throat grew louder, her eyes stared, wide open, she started kicking, screaming, clawing, Steegman and Tereza could hardly control her, she couldn't see them, she was drowning in panic, he heard Tereza shouting for help, yelling for help, while, out of the corner of his eye, he saw the paediatrician running away.

Suddenly the tension ebbed out of her body. She was still, ready to lie down again, she closed her eyes. She gave a deep sigh. Slept.

The paediatrician came running back with a nurse and a needle.

"Look." Steegman pointed at Renée's legs. "She's peed herself."

"That can happen," said the doctor. "The same thing happens with adults in this kind of situation. We've got something for her to wear."

"No," said Tereza, sobbing. "She needed to pee. She wanted to let us know that she had to go to the toilet. She's a big girl now, she didn't want to pee her pants." She covered Renée with her upper body, kissed her on the ear, whispered that it didn't matter, it didn't matter one bit, it was just a little accident.

Then the paediatrician told them that she couldn't make a diagnosis, that there was nothing else she could do for Renée. She'd been in touch with the paediatric intensive care unit at the university hospital in G. A special team was on the way, with an ambulance. Yes, they were coming to fetch her. They'd been informed about Renée's condition.

Steegman helped Tereza to clean her up. She'd pulled herself together, she was talking as if nothing were wrong with Renée. They were at home, in the bathroom, the brightly coloured fish swimming in a line across the window. Hup. There you go. My little sweetheart. My big brave girl.

As he washed his hands, he looked himself deep in the eyes. He thought about all those nightmares he'd had, where, at about this point, even though it wasn't over yet, he'd realised it was actually a nightmare. That was certainly possible, in the seclusion of the hospital lavatories, with this dim lighting . . .

His phone rang, startling him.

Another call from his publisher?

"Emiel? Emiel? Hi! I'm glad I've got hold of you . . . Can you hear me? I'm on the water, I'm on holiday, we're sailing near Capri. Can you hear me O.K.? Did you listen to my message? No? Sit down, Emiel. Are you sitting down? You really need to be sitting down for this . . . Ready? You know the jury of the Golden Belly Band were announcing the shortlist today? Well, you know they didn't release a long list a month and a half ago? Of course you do. Listen. They didn't make a shortlist. There is no shortlist. Do you know why, Emiel? No. Ha, that's one thing you don't know! Well, for the first time in the history of the prize, the judges, in the light of the astounding quality of one particular novel, refused to put together a longlist or a shortlist. According to the press release, the other books didn't deserve the attention! Emiel? This extraordinary turn of events is intended – and I'm quoting here – to honour a truly exceptional book. And the book, Emiel . . . It's *The Murderer*! Emiel, *The Murderer*! I nearly fell overboard! Congratulations, my friend! Emiel? Emiel, listen. The evening news wants to have you on live, there's a camera crew on their way to your house. Are you at home? Where are you, Emiel? Where? The hospital in S.? Z. The hospital in Z. Is that far from your house? The hospital in Z., I'll pass it on. Are you O.K., Emiel? What's that? You don't know? Yeah, I can imagine!"

His publisher congratulated him again on winning the Golden Belly Band and stressed that a live interview on the national evening news programme to celebrate the winner of a literary prize – even the most important one in the country – was not the norm. The exposure would be huge. They needed to strike while the iron was hot, to get all the attention he could. Because tomorrow, and he was sure he didn't need to explain this to Steegman, it would all be over.

TWO

The quick brown fox jumps over the lazy dog.

The reunion is a warm one. The alphabet welcomes me with open arms. This is the right decision. Not writing would be unnatural.

The story of my grandfather on my mother's side. The story of the cudgel, the wooden stick. One day, finally, two men bring electricity to his farm. Towards evening, though, it all goes wrong. One man suddenly becomes stuck to the wire. The other man, quick as a flash, takes the wooden stick they've been carrying around with them all day and whacks his friend on the hand, really hard. He breaks his hand and his wrist, he knocks the man away from the current.

Yesterday I was knocked away from my story as if with a wooden cudgel. T is nowhere to be seen. But if I don't write, I am the dog, curled up in the grass, with events jumping over me, and I may never catch up with the fox.

In the long, bare corridor that connects an old part of the hospital with a new one, I sit with the Olivetti Lettera 32 on my lap, a stylish portable that was very popular with journalists in the 1960s. The sea-green carrying case with its black zip and broad black band across the middle still looks modern even today. In South Vietnam the image must have had all the impact of a flag, of a red cross on a white background: here comes the war correspondent.

Am I reporting from a war zone?

Everything is spinning, whirling, circling, everything is now, present, time is far from past. The fox and the dog are not a fox and not a dog, but two words. There are only words. Every word is a smooth stone sticking up out of the fast-flowing water. We have to get to the other side. There is no way back.

Tereza begs. She is not allowed to travel in the ambulance to G. The experienced nurse explains kindly, patiently, but firmly, why parents are not allowed to travel with the child in such cases: it's for the safety of the child. If something happens, they need to be able to work without interruption. She means: in an emergency situation, hysterical parents in a small space can put their children's lives at risk. She says we should take the time to go home and get a few things. Then we can slowly make our way to the hospital. No hurry. Renée is in the best of hands. She says: you have a wonderful daughter. You'll see her again soon. We'll take good care of her. That's a promise. Tereza asks one more time, please, the nurse doesn't reply but gently holds Tereza's head against her shoulder, just for a moment.

The gesture, unexpected, hits hard. She's acknowledging Tereza's distress, her worry, it's justified, she's the first to admit that this could be bad and that there could be worse to come. At the same time, she's reassuring her. Her gesture shows that Renée really is in the best of hands, she's taking on some of the pain herself, as a woman, perhaps as a mother. By revealing herself to be human, dressed from head in toe in white, she seems like an angel.

We aren't in the house for long. Tereza heads straight upstairs and collects some clothes and toiletries. Bear. Downstairs, in the living room, nothing appears to have changed. It looks staged, a scene devised by someone, the empty cup on the saucer on the arm of the two-seater sofa, a glass espresso cup, the dried ring of foam still smelling bitter sweet. When I look at the black T.V. screen, I see Cavendish, he's sprinting, nose above the front wheel, pulling away from his closest pursuers. The riders have had a headwind all day, the stage is running slowly. Without any delay at all, Renée comes to me and says her leg feels funny. She cries and falls asleep in my arms, in _my_ arms; Daddy's here, she's safe with Daddy. Renée never sleeps in the daytime. I call an ambulance.

Tereza would never have had a coffee.
Never.

The corridor is long, the people walking by are not surprised by the typing. They have ample time to interpret my behaviour, to make up a story. By the time they've reached me, I no longer exist, they glance only at the Olivetti, if at all. Besides, I have the impression that in this place, which connects the ordinary world of cough syrups and sticking plasters to the P.I.C.U., the paediatric intensive care unit, people are quicker to recognise one another.

The cold linearity of the corridor is only reinforced by the two scrawny ficus plants. The plants stand far apart, lonely, it strikes me as a form of abuse. There's art up on the ceiling, illuminated photographs, about one and a half metres square: a canopy of foliage with sunlight streaming through, multiplied by six. A sign on the wall by each of the photos. Hyde Park. Vondelpark. Central Park.

We are the parents of Renée Steegman. We report, as requested, to the A. & E. department at the university hospital, which unlike the one in Z. is bustling with activity. They have one of those machines, like at the butcher's, but we don't need to take a number. There's a television above a drinks machine. Women are playing American football, on a smaller field than the men. They're wearing the same helmets and the rules appear to be the same, but that's not the point: the women are wearing tight shorts and bras. I remember girls jumping up and down on a trampoline on late-night T.V. More of the same, but this time under the guise of sport. Tereza and I sit on the same plastic chairs as the guzzling, gulping primates in the stadium.

The nurse doesn't answer our question, she says the doctor will speak to us. She's friendly, holds the doors open for us. I'm nervous, almost to the point of feeling sick. Tereza and I walk hand in hand along the corridors, following the nurse, our footsteps out of synch. Where's our little girl? We want to see Renée, we can't wait a second longer. It feels as if we're seeing her for the first time, as when she was born. It's as if everything depends on it, that first look, the rest of our lives.

The last time I see someone with a typewriter is in town. From my bench I watch him crossing the large square, dusk, Dekeyser the court bailiff, in his three-quarter length overcoat with its tartan lining. The case in his hand contains a Hermes Baby. The machine has been in his service for twenty-eight years now. His handwriting is illegible and he doesn't trust computers. He says people find the sound soothing and in his profession, in the circles he frequents during the daytime, that can come in handy. He offers me his hipflask, Calvados. An apple a day keeps the doctor away.

Perhaps I'm more bailiff than war correspondent. I note what could be of value. I calm myself.

The P.I.C.U. has seven beds, arranged around a short and long side of a rectangle at the end of the corridor. The nurses' station, with its large windows, is built along the other long side. The nurse says Renée is in Cubicle 4; a bed and all of the surrounding equipment equals one cubicle. The numbers hang from the ceiling, I don't look into the other cubicles, even though a hallowed calmness fills the room – here, too, it's the children's bedtime. The light is dimmed almost everywhere, and the alarm signals that rhythmically intermingle with the chorus of peaceful bleeps

137

are of the soft kind that appear to be a standard part of the heightened state of alert in these surroundings. They remind me of luxurious American family cars, of the friendly, almost apologetic signal informing the driver that the boot is open.

Renée. Something about her face has changed, a certain expression, but otherwise she looks perfectly healthy, with her summery brown skin on the snow-white bedclothes. This is a misunderstanding, a grotesque misunderstanding, someone just needs to break the spell, our little girl is perfectly healthy, we'll take her out of this ridiculously large bed on wheels and go home, we won't bother these people for a moment longer. Tomorrow we'll have a lie-in, by lunchtime we'll be looking back and laughing at this farce. Unbelievable.

We meet Dr De Jager, the head of the department. The nurse who just took a blood sample is Angelique; the one who led us here is Vanessa. It says "A." on Dr De Jager's name badge: Dr A. De Jager. The way she speaks matches her appearance: calm, composed, considered, glancing at Renée as she speaks. She mentions clear indications of decreased consciousness. In addition, there are symptoms of paralysis over the entire right-hand side of her body. But for now they're still in the dark as to the cause. She's received the results of the C.T. scan and E.E.G. from her colleague in Z. In quarter of an hour they'll do an M.R.I. of her brain to get a clear picture of the blood vessels. She'll be lightly anaesthetised, it's of the utmost importance that the patient doesn't move during the period of almost half an hour that the scanner needs to create an image – otherwise the results are blurred and unusable. She talks about magnetic resonance, about the noise, another reason to anaesthetise little children. Then she stops talking. We don't know what to say, our silence is a dumbstruck one. Dr De Jager looks first Tereza in the eyes, then me, and says with deep sympathy: we just have to wait and see.

In the wide corridor in the basement, ten or so golf carts with a multitude of trailers are double parked behind a yellow line. Vanessa tells us that the twelve clinics in this complex are connected by tunnels. Most of them, anyway. More lines and symbols indicate a kind of internal highway code; the smooth, concrete floor, pale green, makes our shoe soles squeak. As soon as we reach the M.R.I. department, everything looks the same as above ground again: the dingy doors, the letters on the signs screwed at right angles to the wall above the doorframe, the tiles. The hip-height Plexiglas panelling.

God exists in things. People no longer believe in the Church, but they do believe in God. God exists in all things – of course God is not a person. Personifying God is completely obsolete. God manifests himself in the art that is produced in His name. In all art. God is nature, mountains, tree frog and cherry tree. Consolation. Beauty. But to whom do all these people appeal in times of need? To a carthorse, a garden snail? To the "Sunflowers" or the "Milkmaid"? They appeal to Him, the One who can intervene, even if His ways are unfathomable, that doesn't matter: help me. What is at stake in these conversations is an adjustment to His diary. Haggling takes place, bartering occurs: if you do this, I'll do that. If you let him live, my lover who's lying on the ground after a V-1 strike, apparently dead, I promise never to see him again – "The End of the Affair".

If God proves too weak to make me believe in Him, how can He be the Almighty?

If God existed, I would believe in Him.

I don't pray, I speak to Renée. I sit in the empty waiting room, I count thirty-seven free chairs. "Your brain doesn't lie," I read on a poster. Photo and slogan allude to the use of polygraphs, but it's about brain research. I don't pray. I encourage her, firmly, urgently, constantly, she has to fight. We are under attack.

Only one parent is allowed in. An airlock entry system with a red flashing light and squawking alarm warns of the powerful electromagnetic field; people with a pacemaker must not go past this point. I watch Tereza walk beside Renée's bed into the examination room, accompanied by Vanessa and Dr De Jager. Just before the doors swing to, I see a man in a dinner jacket walk over to the doctor, pulling his bow tie from the collar of his shirt. I stay behind with a handbag and a jacket. I don't touch the pile of magazines. The reception desk is built of pale-brown bricks, once, I suspect, a temporary solution. Thick bunches of cables dangle from the back of two computers. Post-it notes peel off the keyboard – they won't be read until Monday, when normal business resumes.

I hear the ticking of the seconds on the round railway-station clock. A slight whistling in my nose as I breathe in. I try to talk her round. My concentration could bend a teaspoon.

After twenty minutes, Tereza comes back out, alone, she told them she had to go to the toilet. The radiologist has seen something. She heard him say something to Dr De Jager and he pointed at the screen with his pen. She thinks he said they could stop looking now. She shrugs her shoulders, she has no idea. Another five minutes or so, Vanessa said, then we'll go back upstairs. Tereza shakes her head, her face is grey. They've seen something, she says. It's not good. All I manage to reply is that we have to stay positive. Positive, that's what I come out with, while, inside me, someone is rearranging my organs with both hands.

It's a long way back to the P.I.C.U. Vanessa has shut herself off now, too, or is remaining silent out of sympathy. As soon as Renée is parked in Cubicle 4, Dr De Jager takes us to one side in a room without windows. There's a big desk and a cabinet with a closed shutter. No computer. The surface of the desk is empty.

The M.R.I. scan has provided clarification. It was indeed a stroke. Not a blood clot, but an inflammation of the most important blood vessel in the central part of the left hemisphere of the brain, which has blocked the supply of blood, of oxygen. Vasculitis. The exact cause of the inflammation is still unknown.

141

She pauses for a moment, gives us a chance to catch our breath. Then she says Renée's life is in danger. A medically induced coma is advised in order to halt all activity in the brain. The risk of another cerebral infarction must be minimised. She explains to us that the affected brain cells swell up over time. The compression of other blood vessels can cause a snowball effect, a series of strokes, life-threatening. They're going to insert a probe into her skull so that they can monitor any increase in pressure caused by oedema. That could happen in two, three days' time, when the dead brain cells have reached their maximum extent. If the pressure gets too high, they'll have to operate and remove the top of her skull.

Dr De Jager stops speaking and just sits there on the other side of the desk. She knows the tears will be followed by questions. She gives us plenty of time, her face all warm understanding. I wonder what it must be like for her, in this room without windows, sitting opposite two adults, parents yearning for release, who are hanging on her every word while crumbling in their seats before her very eyes.

No, an operation was, is pointless. With a blood clot, rapid intervention can prevent further disaster, but in Renée's case an operation to clear the obstruction in the blood vessel would do no good. If the brain cells have been without oxygen for any longer than four, five minutes, they die. It's irreversible. Besides, the blood vessel is too deep; surgical intervention could just cause more damage and threaten more vital functions than the consequences of the stroke.

The treatment is currently limited to the administration of
large quantities of corticoids. Cortisone, the inflammation
must be fought. Blood thinners, of course.

After every answer: silence, patience. Disbelief.

If Renée survives this, Dr De Jager doesn't know what condition she'll be in. Not at this stage. The M.R.I. shows the
initial stages of damage in the central section on the left;
they anticipate that the damage will be more extensive. It'll
only become clearly visible later, as the dead cells swell.
The affected area controls the motor functions of the right
half of the body and her speech. We have to wait and see.
We have to wait and see if she'll be able to swallow, to blink.
If her loss of eyesight is temporary, related to the trauma,
or structurally connected to the brain damage.

We can stay a few more minutes, but then Vanessa and
Angelique need to get to work. We look at Renée in that
big bed. Her face is relaxed. A little girl of nearly four
years old, asleep. The thought that somehow the M.R.I. has
malfunctioned, that in some or other inexplicable way a
mistake has been made: bubbles that burst apart before
they even start to float. Other girls of nearly four have
broken a leg at a birthday party today. It could have been
a leg. An arm. She could have been sleeping between the
two of us now, the brand-new plaster over that soft downy
fluff. Flowers and hearts. And kisses, lots of kisses, from
the bottom to the top, like a zip. That's what could have
happened.

She has to stay alive, says Tereza in the car. It is a command,
the emphasis on "has to". The command is directed both at
Renée and at the two of us. A solemn resolution, a promise,
a magic spell. She has to stay alive. We are on our way to
her mother's, who lives five minutes from the hospital. As
of tomorrow night we can sleep in a room in the paediatric
ward. We have to stay nearby, but we also need to sleep,
says Vanessa as she walks us outside. Renée is going to
need us, so we have to be there for her. It's a comforting
command. I hope that one day I will have to be there for
Renée, who has had to stay alive.

We're lying together in Eva's bed – Eva's the teenage
daughter of Tereza's mother's partner – staring into the
semi-darkness. It's strange to see our sadness in others
for the first time; it is just as big, which really moves me.
Tereza calls Vanessa every hour, we can phone whenever
we want. Renée is stable. Her condition hasn't changed.
Vanessa warned us about later, when we go back in, because
Renée is now connected to the ventilator and other equipment. Apparently it's a sight that could shock us, even now.
I think back to our car journey, not even twenty-four hours
ago, Renée in the back, singing, laughing. Not one warning
sign, however small, that somewhere in the network of her
kilometres of veins the blood is having difficulty flowing.
Whenever she laughs, she gets the hiccups, has done ever
since she was born, since she first laughed. It must be something to do with her diaphragm, some harmless design flaw.
It's the confluence of events, thinking about her hiccuping
laugh and the callous indifference of the early blackbird near

our window as it launches into its dazzling song, amplified by the courtyard garden, heralding another glorious summer's day: I feel my face change, and I laugh. Nothing more than a little puff of air expelled from my nose, a twitch of the muscles around my mouth and eyes. Then it's over and I think about the blackbird's hormonally controlled brain, which makes it such a virtuoso, all to defend its chances of offspring, varying on the same theme with mathematical exhaustion; a brain no bigger than a chickpea.

Go on, I hear Tereza's mother whisper. Just go to your baby. It's still night in the house, Tereza doesn't want to leave without saying anything. She sticks her head into the bedroom, her mother asks if we've had breakfast, the table's laid. No? She'll cook tonight. Just an hour, and then we can go back. We have to eat, don't we? We'll see them this afternoon, we'll have to think about it. Just go now.

"Your baby." It echoes in my mind. She could call Renée by her name, but she doesn't. It's most probably coincidence, or perhaps it shows great understanding. A warm blanket that she wraps around Tereza, Renée and me, inseparably connecting us.

There's no traffic on the roads in the city. On the pavements, the zombies are leaving the medieval centre after the first Saturday night of the ten-day city festival. Young people, big children. Some of them look up, but they don't see us. Their survival instinct has kicked in, they keep moving, on their way back to their lair.

145

The P.I.C.U. has a remote-controlled door with a window, to be opened only after visual identification of a visitor by a nurse or doctor. We see Vanessa in the nurses' station, she indicates that we can come through, that she'll be there in a moment, she puts her thumb up. I can see it in Tereza's reaction – she can't hold herself back, she's walking a couple of metres ahead of me – I notice how her longing to see Renée is instantly crushed by new impressions. My thought: a spaceship. An illuminated mother ship with the small creature on the bed in sharp contrast. Curious aliens have seized her, penetrated her, nose, mouth, arms, hands, even somewhere beneath the sheets. She is at their mercy. Her skull: a tube with wiring has been inserted into a shaved, red strip between forehead and crown, as if her comatose dreams are being tapped. She already seems a bit like one of them. Bear, startled, against her cheek, looks on through scratched eyes.

I saw my father cry only once, almost twenty years ago, at my grandmother's funeral. I call him on the phone, it's half past seven on a Sunday morning, he knows something's wrong. At first he keeps trying to find words to say, but as my own words eat their way into his heart, he falls silent. My mother's voice, she's crying before I can even say hello. She doesn't let me finish speaking, asks if Renée's going to be alright. I'm sitting on a bench, outside, I look at Tereza's hand on my knee. It's a beautiful morning. Her hand is completely relaxed, it rests on my knee. The light. If I were a painter, this hand would be enough for me. Is Renée going to be alright, my mother repeats. It's as if everything suddenly depends on me. I hesitate to reply: what if it really

146

does suddenly depend on me, a moment of grace? Can I bring myself not to answer "yes", not to try it? Can I bring myself to lie to my mother? Silently, I curse to myself. I hesitate, first I hesitate, then I wait for my mother, for her to say "Emiel?", or "Are you still there?", or just "Hello?" If I wait, the chance of a question coming that I can answer with "yes" is practically one hundred per cent. I just need to make my "yes" sound as if, strictly speaking, it could actually be a belated response to the previous question.

I keep a constant eye on the meter with the red digits. I sit in a chair that's too low for Renée's elevated bed. Angelique has shown us that they've set an upper limit; if the pressure goes over that limit, a loud alarm will sound. It's terrible, I can't not look at the digits for any longer than five seconds. We don't want to leave anything to chance. We have nothing else to do. What could be more important? How can anyone expect Tereza and me not to sit by the bed like highly strung watchdogs? Two bright red numbers are now the centre of our existence, a clearly visible, scientifically determined indicator of our fate. It has never been simpler. It is a horror.

We take turns. I drink Cécémel, chocolate milk, the other drinks in the machine seem too summery, too cheerful. I haven't drunk chocolate milk for ages, even though we've often had it in the house these past few years. I feel the ice-cold, syrupy chocolate milk slide down deep into my stomach. It could be thirty years ago. I suck greedily on the straw, like a child finding the nipple. I could light up a cigarette, have a strong drink, it's allowed. It's something

147

men would do, if this were a film. In a film, I'd be sitting in a bar now, but in a book I'm not so sure. Would the author come up with the idea of thrusting a chocolate milk into my hands if he hadn't himself been in a situation similar to mine and stood in front of a drinks machine in the deserted waiting room of an intensive care unit? Yes, I think so. I think I'd come up with something like that. It wouldn't result in a very dramatic scene. I'd have to smash something. As I slurped the last drops of chocolate milk from the carton, I'd have to lash out at something, with all my strength, all my emotion.

Tereza and I turn into something like travel guides. We collect our family members from the main entrance of Clinic 12 and lead them through lifts, corridors, sliding and swinging doors to Renée. We explain what's happened, a story we quickly polish down to its essence, embellished with a few dramatic details, and we give a prognosis, what's going to happen in the worst-case and best-case scenarios. It's a lot to take in, the image and the words. For them it's as if this is all happening only now, now that they're seeing their Renée in this bed. It's strange, but after the visits, in the waiting room or the cafeteria, where we have a quick chat afterwards, Tereza and I can both feel it: we are a day ahead of them. Our sorrow seems a day older. More mature.

Not Vanessa, not Angelique, but Deborah is now taking care of Renée. Which is strange, because Angelique is still here, still on duty. She smiles at us as she walks past Cubicle 4, but differently, literally distant. I don't understand. Deborah is a fine nurse, but why assign her to Cubicle 4

when Angelique's used to the situation and already knows Renée a bit? Deborah's tall, with blonde curls and white glasses. She's decorated her Crocs – rubbery sandals that appear to have been manufactured for use on a slippery pebble beach, but which have become a standard part of nurses' uniforms – with flowers and frogs, studs specially made for these shoes. Angelique is a Mediterranean type, small, dark, sturdy – young, all of them are young. Angelique wears her heart on her sleeve. The way she dealt with Renée was sweet and gentle, stroking her arm, squeezing her hand, talking to her like a mother. Why take her away from Renée? Tereza laughs a little at my question; isn't it obvious? Angelique, and the other nurses, are protected by regularly assigning them to different patients. There's a constant risk of developing too close an emotional connection with a particular child when they've been providing them with intensive care for three, four shifts in a row. Children here, in the P.I.C.U., are children who either leave very soon for another part of the hospital, or who pass away.

It's after seven in the evening when we meet Dr Verryckt. She's Dr De Jager's colleague, they run the P.I.C.U. together. Whichever one has the night shift sleeps at the hospital, on a weekly rotation. She's perched against Renée's bed. Physically, she's the same kind of woman as Dr De Jager, as if it's a prerequisite for this job. She leaves her lab coat hanging open. She's wearing white plimsolls and jeans and a plain cotton sweater with a high, scooped neck. She's not wearing any make-up, not because she's working tonight, but because she never uses make-up. Some women can't

take make-up. They never become a painting, you still see them as a canvas with paint on it – a waste of both. Dr Verryckt has those white subcutaneous skin bumps around her eyes, in her case they make her look younger, as if they were freckles. I imagine she looked just the same when she was a sixteen-year-old. It makes it seem as if she's got into the habit of firmly crossing her arms when speaking to parents only so as to emphasise her authority. I take an immediate liking to her. There's something disarming about her. For now the cause of the inflammation remains unknown. They've sent a number of samples to the lab, which will give us a better idea in a few days' time.

Otherwise everything's fine with her blood clotting. She points at the mother ship and says they've found a good balance between the anaesthesia and the medication. We have to remain cautious, but it's not a bad sign that the pressure today has risen by only a few units. She'd expected more, yes. We mustn't forget that it's still early, but it's not a bad start. Her favourite phrase is: a lot of. A lot of research, a lot of patience. She refuses to respond to our direct questions about Renée's future. There's still a lot of guesswork, it's too soon. She says she's seen me in the waiting room, or rather heard me. She nods at the Olivetti beside my chair. She imagines Renée is very familiar with the sound. If I like, I can type here, at her bedside. Then Renée can hear me writing, like at home. I feel as if I can't hold it in any longer, I look down at the floor, I want to kiss her, this woman. She says, I saw you on the news. She says, the two of you must try to get some sleep tonight.

The little room in the paediatric ward in Clinic 6 isn't much to look at. At the end of a corridor, smaller than the other rooms, a storeroom for mattresses and rolling stock. I help two nurses with the removal work. There's room for a fold-up bed on the left and the right, with a bedside cabinet in between. The layout is fixed, the beds have to remain apart, this is a place for sleeping. We're too tired to feel insulted, us, having wild, screaming sex, while our daughter's in a coma? We get the message, the precaution, we don't feel targeted, we're grateful for the place to stay. The clinics were built in the 1970s, ugly, uniform, colourless, the same aluminium frames have been used throughout the buildings, to make walls for rooms, for instance, filled in at the bottom with grey board, with frosted glass above. We can hear the boy in the next room breathing.

Waking up. It's the first time. We turn off the nightlight with a slight feeling of hope. Dr Verryckt has given us a boost. Just a few more hours and Renée will have survived this day. She's fighting. We'll know more tomorrow. I sleep without dreaming. I am briefly absent, for two, three hours. For that short while, nothing has happened. And then I wake up in the university hospital, on a camp bed, and it's all happening again. I jump up, startled by the first bite of ink-black grief: it's ravenous, it's been waiting for me for hours. It feels like a panic attack in an aeroplane, a fall into ice-cold water: I have to get out! Tereza's already sitting beside me on the bed, trying to hold me down, hold me in. I can hear them, the sounds I'm producing, repellent sounds that would normally make me stop, deeply ashamed, but I have no space, no time, my self-awareness can only watch, powerless. I go under, I am sinking, I cling to Tereza, who doesn't try to calm me, but encourages me. I realise I've never cried before, that I've always managed to stop. I open up, I make space, for one blissful moment losing myself in loss is a sort of gain. Then it ebbs away and empty exhaustion follows.

This crying is not without risks; it is never without consequences. At some point, I don't know exactly when, but sometime during the raging storm: something snapped. – No, wrong word, the cliché doesn't fit. Came lose, something is adrift. It's floating through my body, it's physical. I couldn't point to where it once belonged. It's always in the wrong place. It won't stop me from doing anything, but everything I do, or don't do, from now on, it will be there, in yet another, wrong place.

In the long corridor to the P.I.C.U. we've got into the habit of touching the wooden sticks that hold the ficuses upright in their pots. We can't not do it now, says Tereza. They won't let us in yet, they're washing Renée. Through the window in the door we see a new nurse at work in Cubicle 4. Peggy has a moustache, it goes perfectly with her surly attitude. She doesn't show any sense of involvement. Ugly hands, coarse, she seems too fierce for this ward. Our defence mechanisms kick in. We check everything we've learned about the mother ship. I watch the dripping of the various catheters. We look at the settings of the medicine pumps, with their American alarms, syringes filled with medication slowly squeezed into a tube by a pump, and note the rate at which the medicine is administered. We peer under the covers at her groin, to make sure there's no blood in the drip tube. After a few minutes, calm descends once more, we kiss Renée, manoeuvring our faces between the tubes to get as close to her as possible. I kiss her next to the probe on her skull. Tereza strokes balm onto her dry lips with the tip of her little finger. With one hand, with my thumb, I gently massage the soles of her feet. The pressure has risen by one unit, five away from the limit.

Again and again I'm hurled back to those two endless hours. I apologise to my daughter. I see the man with the beard, Mieke, her mother. Will I ever get up from that orange sofa? The longer I think about it, the greater my sense of bewilderment. I feel my fingernails pressing into my palms, as if I'm attacking myself with my motionless fists. I press harder, want to pierce my skin, but my nails aren't long enough, too blunt. Ridiculous. As if that would change anything, as if some pathetic demonstration of self-hatred could exonerate me. Dr De Jager can say what she likes, as clearly as she wants: no, this couldn't have been prevented, the blood vessel closes off and that's that, operating was not an option – and still all the doctors in the world won't be able to pull me up off that sofa.

They've given us a badge so we can get a discount on food in the cafeteria. We want to have breakfast but, as we enter, a waitress in a faded apron and a messy hairnet picks up the tray of rolls and carries it through to the back. When she reappears, she says: breakfast stops at nine thirty. She doesn't even look at us. There's a digital clock above the till.

It's 9.26. I say we'd like breakfast, it's not half past nine yet. I can see at a glance that, for the woman, it's just a question of fetching bread and taking money – everything else is in the refrigerated counters, we'll eat in the dining room and then return our own trays to the clearing station. All she has to do is fetch some bread and take our money. We're setting up for lunch, she says haughtily. Her colleagues are sitting at the cafeteria tables, all of them in hairnets, about fifteen women leaning back lazily, having expertly stuffed their faces. Now she's allowed to have her breakfast – no, it's not half nine yet, but by half nine she wants to be sitting down, yes, she's earned it, we're not going to spoil it for her, everyone knows it stops at half nine, some people still try it on, but not with her, if you give in just once, where will it end? That is what she conveys to us by the way she removes the remaining crumbs of bread. We'd like to have breakfast, says Tereza. Sorry for the inconvenience. We have a badge. We didn't know breakfast finished at half past nine. She snatches the badge from Tereza's hand, gives it a filthy look, front and back. Tosses the badge identifying us as long-term visitors, here with a seriously ill family member, onto the stainless steel beside the cash register and dismissively traipses through to the back. My legs are shaking, Tereza gives me a nudge and says, go and sit down.

A pathetic poxy witch who's packed full of shit right up to her earholes; they're all full of shit, the whole lot of them, with their crappy, petty dramas and she-borrowed-two-cigarettes-from-me-and-didn't-give-them-back, or she-knew-I-wanted-holiday-then-but-she-still-went-and-put-in-a-request-anyway, or I-did-this-or-that-again-yesterday-and-that-cow's-never-even-done-it-once, overstaffed but still complaining until they run out of breath, always indignant about something, it's all too much for them, oh poor me, lugging their massive arses around like great big bin bags full of cottage cheese and their saggy udders oozing with used chip fat, their gobsmacking egocentrism, the stupidity that drips, thick as porridge, from their dense, swollen heads. Stinking waste-disposal units for worthless sperm. The evolutionary dregs, not good enough to feed to pigs. Line them up against the wall, without a blindfold. Johnny's mother had three sons: Bing, Bong and . . .

The man must be a doctor or an experienced nurse. But the shopping trolley he's pushing around turns that impression on its head. Wanted: homeless man. Experience with shopping trolleys required. In-house training. Every day he follows the same route, from one patient on artificial respiration to the next. His worldly goods consist of a few thick plates and various X-rays of lungs that are vulnerable to infection. He is skilled, just as a homeless man is in the art of survival. A routine radiologist, silently and unobtrusively roaming the hospital. Is it the shopping trolley that makes him move differently from other doctors? Has it gradually robbed him of his status? Do people shun him, is he a walking example of the fate that can befall even a highly trained doctor? Is the squeaky left front wheel like a rattle sounding a warning of disease? He drinks, secretly, halfway down the long corridors in the shelter of his high shoulders, he can't stand the dirty looks anymore. He's fired. He stops leaving the house, never gets up off the sofa, and that drives his wife away. One day a man in a three-quarter length overcoat with a tartan lining sits typing at his dining table. When he's finished, they leave the house together.

It's an amazing illusion: the more I write, the better Renée gets. Saving her by typing words on paper. I type blindly, hunting for small changes in her face, in her heart rate. I'd like to believe that the sound excites her at first and then, for a long time, soothes her. Is she weaving the sounds into her deep, shadowy dreams? The bell, does the bell make her happy? Will this be her first, untraceable memory, the cheerful ting of the Lettera 32? Will she, long after my death, find the typewriter and inexplicably start weeping with happiness when she hears the bell?

We try to shut ourselves off from everything that happens outside of Cubicle 4. Gradually the suffering of other children and parents seeps through to us. The door to the nurses' station is always open. At quiet moments, the preparation and collection of medicines, topping up the bandages and towels and disinfectants, we can hear the nurses talking to one another. The open door works like an acoustic mirror, the sound that leaves the nurses' station is channelled around the corner and straight into Cubicle 4. Vanessa gave the lawn a quick mow yesterday evening. Angelique has raspberry jam with her breakfast every day. Melissa has tried to make lasagne, this news causes quiet hilarity. Cubicle 2 is a torn stomach lining with blood in the faeces. Cubicle 3 concussion. And then there's Cubicle 6, which speaks for itself. The girl of about eight was hit outside her house by a drunk driver. Months ago she arrived here, torn to pieces. Now she's still in pieces and pissed off and defiant. What we hear, always in bursts of a few minutes, is an unnaturally slow and drawn-out "shiiiit". It could be funny, a girl of eight swearing like a trooper. But not here. Not if that's all she can manage with all of her strength, before falling asleep, exhausted.

The pressure hasn't risen since this morning. We're almost forty-eight hours after the stroke and it's still five units below the upper limit. We don't dare to ask the doctors anything, we don't want to crush our budding hope with our own hands. We haven't seen any major fluctuations, we think we can assume that the pressure, if it rises, will increase uniformly, at the same rate as it has done so far. If we have just one more day to go in the danger zone and the past thirty-six hours have seen a rise of just three units, is it unreasonable to hope? She will stay alive. Tereza and I are no longer in any doubt. Renée is stubborn. She's fighting. The pressure is stable. We hug each other and we talk about this gift, our new Renée. We are going to have a new Renée, not like other children, an extraordinary little girl, we'll give her an even warmer welcome than we did the first time. Our love has multiplied, couldn't be bigger. Every time we enter the P.I.C.U., we are stepping into a maternity ward, making our way to a cradle. She's so beautiful. It was already there within her name: she would be reborn, her new life was predestined. Our future with her rolls out in front of us like a red carpet. We have been chosen. Other people will envy us.

Visiting hours. My father collapses at the bedside of his

only grandchild. The sight of that bald strip and the probe in the skull, all the activity through nose and mouth, the intimidating surroundings, I want to be understanding, but suddenly I feel incapable. He's crying as if it's a deathbed, after Tereza and I explained it all to him in the waiting room, shared our first, fragile hope with him and my mother. It's as if they didn't hear us, deafened by grief that refuses to evolve, that has stubbornly taken root in the shocking news of a stroke. Oh, not Renée, I hear him wailing. Afterwards, too, in the cafeteria, I can't get through to him. She's not even four years old, he says, shaking his head, defeated. I put a lid on my rising irritation, he's not doing it on purpose. I just want him to show some consideration for us, as we are for him. I'd be surprised if he expects us to have the strength to deal with his stubborn grief, but if we make the attempt, a little cooperation would be appreciated.

An hour or so later, Marie, my sister, is sticking up for him. He's a sensitive man, always has been. I tell her I am, too. She says they've got some catching up to do. That's only natural and she knows how he feels. Tereza and I are living at the hospital, sitting at her bedside for hours; our parents just saw their grandchild for the second time, for only a few minutes. I shouldn't be too hard on them. I say I'm not being hard at all. I say I don't want any weeping and wailing at her bedside, not even any silent tears. Tears aren't going to do Renée any good at all. What she needs is people talking, familiar voices, soothing sounds, we have to think about her, not about our own sadness. That's for at home, and even there preferably in the dark. In front of the mirror, if you have to. Renée is alive. There won't be any mourning for her. Marie sips her tea with lemon and says it's only natural for me to be angry. I say I'm not angry. If I were angry, really angry, then you wouldn't be sipping your tea and then saying, yes, it's only natural for me to be angry. You know, if I were really angry, that I'd explode. If you really thought I was angry, you'd never speak to me like that. She lays her hand on mine, says, you're right. Smiling, she looks at the other tables and says, you're always right. Instantly we're teenagers in Zingene again: I thump her on the shoulder and she thumps me back, far too hard, so I have to thump her again.

When we're forty and thirty-six again, she tentatively asks if she can congratulate me. On the Golden Belly Band. I shrug. Of course she can. She hasn't seen the news item yet, someone told her about it, described it. Of course she can congratulate me. She says she received a few phone calls yesterday. A few – nine to be precise. She let Mum and Dad know right away, they only answer calls from known numbers, the same as her. The clip's on YouTube, all the newspapers have a link on their homepage. She asks if I saw the papers this morning.

The pressure hasn't changed all day. Her heart rate, blood pressure, everything's stable. It's all under control. Tereza has gone to bed, I sit there for a while. In the P.I.C.U., too, it's quiet: no new patients, no new crises, all the sounds are familiar. For the first time since Saturday, I feel my body relax. It's ten o'clock, I know I'm going to sleep soundly, I enjoy holding it off, the feeling of my eyes closing is enough. I realise there's no safer place for Renée than here.

Surrounded by the best care. I feel – it's a strange sensation – at home in the paediatric intensive care unit at the heart of the university hospital. I hope Renée can hear me typing. When I'm not typing, I'm whispering in her ear. I tell her about my Mr Owl when I was small. I hope she has a Mr Owl of her own, with two glowing eyes, to keep her company in the darkness.

It's taken me this long to notice. Bear has been a constant presence for almost four years but only now do I see he's been patched up on the left-hand side of his head – it's like a plaster! Are all teddy bears born that way? He's lying under her paralysed arm, apparently afraid to move, and he has a head injury, just like Renée. If that's right, then why are teddy bears born in such a sorry state? To arouse the sympathy of heartless toddlers? Were they originally healthy and whole, but, as cuddly toys didn't used to be that cheap and yet had to put up with years of rough treatment, were they constantly being patched up, so creating the image that's imitated as standard nowadays? Or is this just one of those breathtaking twists of fate?

After I've given her a goodnight kiss and said goodbye to the nurses, I'm the only person in the corridors of Clinic 12. A man could make himself very scared by walking along the fluorescently illuminated corridors of a deserted Clinic 12 at about eleven at night. I try to keep my echoing footsteps rhythmic, not to look over my shoulder, to give the swinging doors time to close behind my back. When I get outside, I can't shake off that feeling of unease. The paediatric ward, in Clinic 6, is a hundred metres away, on the other side of an expanse of grass, beside the multistorey car park. The hospital grounds are silent, there are no cars on the streets, it feels like something's wrong with my ears, as if I've just stepped out of some infernal din. The dark-grey night sky – above the city the sky is never black – is a bell jar, shutting out every sound. I am alone. I click my tongue, and can hear it, but just in front of my face the sound disappears, is smothered. Everything I see is bathed in the eerie, shadowy orange of the sodium street lights. I am a miniature of myself, standing in a model of the hospital complex in front of the entrance to Clinic 12. The rabbits on the grass don't move. For the first time, I can imagine what agoraphobia might feel like. Crossing a practically empty lawn of that size feels like an impossible task. So I don't take the shortest route to Clinic 6. I follow the road, the route the cars take. The cycle paths have recently been sprayed with red paint, it stinks of chemicals. The road markings are also new. I don't walk on the narrow footpath, but on the tarmac. When I reach the multistorey car park, there's a red, octagonal traffic sign on my right, with four white capital letters on it: STOP. I'm sure I've never really noticed this sign before. There's no doubt who the message is aimed at. I halt in front of the white line on the road surface. To the right, I can see a long way, to the left there's a black hole: a sharp bend around the corner of the building. Any car taking this curve carelessly could hit me. But I can't hear anything, no engine, there are no cars around: I know it's not actually possible, but still I know I'll have to be quick, as quick as I can. It's like a film by David Lynch – I know there's a car around the corner, waiting for me to cross.

The fire extinguishers. Two identical, heavy cylinders, next to each other above the foot of Tereza's bed. Spares. Fire hoses are provided at various points throughout the corridors of the paediatric ward. I lie close to Tereza, against her back, I try to encircle her, from the crown of her head, with the underside of my chin, to her toes, with the insteps of my feet, a warm shell, made to fit. The silent crying soon stops. I'm lying with my hip on the iron frame of the camp bed, but I stay there for a little longer to make sure Tereza's asleep, that the pain has eased, I wait for a deep sigh. I remember thinking yesterday that the fire extinguishers reminded me of something. When was the last time I thought about fire? I can feel the memory taking shape and trying to break through to my consciousness, I recently thought about fire – smoke! That was it: smoke. I see the woman with long curly hair at the end of the row of chairs. A waiting room, people are reading magazines, playing with their phones. The woman doesn't know she's the subject of an experiment and she's being filmed. Smoke suddenly comes rising from under the door. The woman notices it immediately and looks at the others, who go on reading and playing. The woman stays where she is, even as the smoke becomes thicker, she's right in the middle of it, there's clearly a fire on the other side of the door, but she stays sitting there because no-one else seems concerned. Peer pressure. Allowing your behaviour to depend on how a group of your peers acts in a given situation. Afterwards, the woman claps her hands over her mouth. She was dying to run away, but she didn't want to be the first. There was a fire two metres away from her, but she was afraid of looking like a fool.

*

Can the situations be compared? Renée never sleeps in the daytime, and yet I sit there on an orange sofa with her on my lap and I don't do a thing. Am I that easy to switch off? Is a table of strangers all it takes? What kind of father consigns his daughter of nearly four to the flames?

It's just before ten on Tuesday morning when Dr Verryckt reports to Cubicle 4. She's come to answer the question we still haven't dared to ask: she doesn't anticipate any intracranial oedema forming now. They won't be opening up Renée's skull. The hole they drilled to get the probe in will close up by itself. The good news makes us greedy, but we'll have to wait for the next M.R.I. scan, scheduled for tomorrow, for more answers. It's just before ten thirty on Tuesday morning when Dr Verryckt is pleased to inform us of a change in the schedule: a slot for a scan has become free, this afternoon at three. The excitement goes to our heads. They say bad luck comes in threes – could the same apply to good luck? Is that so absurd? If, over the course of the generations, one can become a commonly accepted wisdom, is it so absurd to suspect its implicit corollary might also apply? No oedema, an early scan, and therefore answers sooner than expected; if we have any right to a third helping of good luck, it can only involve those answers. If Saturday was an unlucky day, today can be our lucky day. Tereza and I talk with some caution, but is it really so absurd? No, we don't think so. We feel strong. We have become stronger. We won't simply allow ourselves to be pigeonholed along with our misfortune.

The basement is full of activity now. The electric carts are driving up and down the tunnels and corridors. Some of them are towing as many as five trailers, dirty washing in big laundry bags, piled up between tall mesh sides. The speeds are impressive, and the carts pulling beds and patients go just as swiftly. It's like something from an old-fashioned sci-fi movie. Renée's bed has landed on a busy space station. Or we've found our way through a hidden entrance in a fjord to the secret lair of some villainous billionaire with megalomaniacal ambitions, in an early James Bond film.

The people in the waiting room are very understanding. Couples, elderly folk. Neat clothes, combed hair, clean shoes. Renée is steered straight into the squawking airlock. It's all according to schedule, but makes it seem as if we've been given priority. As I look for somewhere to sit, I hear people saying they don't mind. It's so awful to see a little child being wheeled in. One woman has to take three trains to get back to K., but when she sees those little mites coming past in their beds, she doesn't mind waiting a bit longer. She can always catch a later train, can't she? Those poor little lambs. Her voice is so loud that I think for a moment she's trying to force me to express my gratitude, that I'm being obliged to show some sign of acknowledgement, humility in the face of all that compassion for her fellow human beings – I am a jerk. The woman isn't expecting anything at all.

It's incredible that I was sitting here on my own on Saturday evening. It seems like an eternity ago. It feels like a second chance. I try to act differently, calmly, less emotionally. I have to show faith that there'll be a good result, have to be strong. Why do we persist, in such circumstances, in thinking we can have the slightest influence on the way things will turn out? I talk to Renée, calmly; I tell her everything's going to be alright. I say that the din of the scanner will soon be over and we'll see each other again before long. It's impossible for me not to talk to Renée.

I see Evelyne and Peggy emerge first. When she's uncoupled from the mother ship, moving Renée is a logistical feat. The two of them keep a close eye on cables, tubes, catheter stands and mobile apparatus.

Evelyne tells me Renée's done well – whatever that's supposed to mean. She says it in that typical nurse's tone, firm and patronising, Renée's listening too. Tereza follows after the bed. With one look she tells me she hasn't found out anything new. I join the procession, we are the parents of this sick child, as everyone can see. They look at us, trying to assess the gravity of the situation. We're like a motorway pile-up, irresistible.

Dr Verryckt is perching, rather awkwardly this time, on the edge of Renée's bed. Evelyne is still busy docking the bed with the mother ship. Dr De Jager stands beside Dr Verryckt, holding a folder in front of her stomach. They've evidently decided Dr Verryckt will do the talking, here, not in the little office without a computer: a good sign. But the fact that there are two of them is a bad sign, outweighing the good. Aware of our intense focus on what she's about to say, Dr Verryckt briefly picks at her nose. I don't dare to look, I hope nothing comes dangling from her nose, that the news we're about to hear, the memory of it, won't forever be associated with that image. Is it because I can't quite bring myself to look at her that she becomes aware of the danger and, with a quick wipe of her finger, puts a stop to her picking? She slides half of her hands into the tight pockets of her jeans and crosses one white plimsoll over the other, and I know from the way her mouth hangs open for a moment before she speaks that it's bad, that it's not what we've been hoping for.

The damage we could see on Saturday has, as expected, spread. However, it's still within the same limited area. Dr De Jager will show us the scans in a minute. The damage is extensive. It's the area that controls all the muscles in the right-hand side of the body, and the speech. Her motor functions and speech are gone for now. They're still not sure what condition she'll be in when she comes out of this; her recovery's going to depend on her character, her willpower, and also on the way her brain develops, on the extent to which the healthy parts take over. But there's no chance of a complete recovery, that much is clear. Even after a long period of rehabilitation, there'll still be substantial residual damage.

Tereza and I sit staring at the floor like a pair of whipped dogs. I've had plenty of time to study the floor in the P.I.C.U. Plastic, possibly old-fashioned lino, with a hardwearing top layer for intensive use, easy to clean, as it's laid in large sections, with only a few joins for the dirt to pile up in, traditionally speckled with white, green and grey to imitate the chips of marble in terrazzo flooring. To my surprise, I hear Tereza tentatively ask if Renée is out of danger now. No, that's not the case. She's no longer at risk of oedema, no. But until she can breathe on her own, she isn't out of danger. Until she wakes up from her coma. Sometimes it happens really quickly, sometimes it takes weeks, sometimes longer. It's impossible to predict. The body doesn't wake up until it's ready. They'll gradually reduce the anaesthesia. Dr De Jager informed us on Saturday about the possibility of blindness. That's why, says Dr Verryckt, it's important for us to stay nearby: when Renée wakes up, she has to be able to hear one of us.

When we've sat in silence for a while, Dr V. puts her hand on Tereza's knee and says she'll leave us alone for a bit now.

What happens after that will stay with me for a long time. We're limp rags, Tereza and I; at first we don't even have the strength to look at each other, to speak or to comfort. I want to stop, I don't want to be me anymore. I want to leave this body that's filled with pitch-black nothingness. There's nothing left for me in Emiel Steegman now. And I realise that I could do it: a bed, a blanket, a few minutes in the darkness of my closed eyes – a realisation like a redemptive resolution. Then a man comes into the waiting room, he's pulling a trolley loaded with cans of drink for the machine. He gives us a nod, takes the huge ring of keys from his belt and opens the door of the machine.

Could the man in the waiting room be God? Perhaps he

appears just once in a person's life, a cameo. Maybe He's not in everything, not in everything at once, but very occasionally just in one single thing. Never by request, not a trained monkey.

There's nothing remarkable about it. But that's exactly what makes it remarkable: because essentially it amounts to nothing. With his back towards Tereza and me, the man refills the machine. We watch. There really is nothing else to report. When the man has finished and he vanishes just as he appeared, his actions mirrored, the north and south poles have switched places, and all that pitch-black nothingness now has a different charge: peace. I can think of no better word. First there was nothing, then, without our noticing the transition, there's boundless peace with whatever is to come. I don't understand how it's possible. But that's what happens. The machine has been filled, and we are at peace.

On Tuesday night Vanessa, the head nurse, decides on her own initiative to allow Renée to breathe by herself for an hour. No problems occur. Afterwards Renée is very tired, her heart rate drops below sixty.

We try to prepare ourselves. How will we be able to calm our little girl if she wakes up in the pitch dark, half paralysed and unable to speak? How can we explain to her what's going on? How will we ease the claustrophobic panic, which threatens to seize me by the throat in her stead? Dr De Jager says Renée won't remember anything about the stroke. She probably won't remember Amélie's birthday party, or the rest of that Saturday or the days before. Not at first. This is a recurring pathology, a reflex of the system, stress-related, self-protective: temporary amnesia. Like fainting.

We have constant physical contact, we talk to her through our skin. They advise us to stroke her right arm and leg in particular. She is paralysed, but hasn't lost her sense of feeling. The more we stimulate that side, even now, the better. The rehabilitation has begun.

An M.R.I. scan does what, at one time, was done for real: it cuts the brain into thin slices, like a ball of Edam cheese. Now it's virtual, magnetic, every slice a photograph. Projecting them in rapid succession creates the illusion of a moving image, something taking place before our very eyes, but which we can't possibly be witnessing – it's as if we're watching the Lumière brothers' very first show: we're travelling through our child's brain, from top to bottom, and back again. Those unreachable treasure chambers are exposed. The gaping darkness of the ones that have been plundered of their precious cells, flooded with sterile fluid, serum, traces of wanton violence to the cerebral cortex. Then a 3D image of the complex network of secret passageways, like the branches of a tree. The symmetry with the central section of the right half no longer exists, the tiny veins are gnarled, twisted, fragile. In spite of this nanoprecision, the image is unable to distinguish between scar tissue from an infection and a congenital anomaly – congenital, not genetic. Only a biopsy or an image taken before the stroke could provide a conclusive answer, and neither is an option. The truth is locked away. Only sixteen similar cases are known in Europe, with twenty-three cases in the United States and Canada combined. This sort of cerebral infarction in a child of almost four, it's like the lottery: a chance of one in tens of millions. Statistically speaking, the doctors have little to go on, there are too few cases for them to be able to assert anything with confidence. What her future has to offer neurologically is statistically unknown.

On Wednesday, after she has breathed largely independently from three in the afternoon until eleven at night, and her blood is absorbing oxygen well, they decide to proceed to "extubation" on Thursday morning. It's a risky undertaking, she hasn't been given any food – by Nutricia, the manufacturers of Cécémel – through her nasal drip since midnight so as to prevent vomit ending up in the respiratory tract during the procedure, in which case the ventilator has to go straight back into the windpipe. Everyone gathers around the bed; we are sent to the waiting room. We lean against the drinks machine, the high frequency of the vibrating motor, a buzzing that's like hearing and feeling at the same time, filling our ribcages, which are pressed tightly together. Five minutes later, we see Vanessa's beaming face – come on in. Renée's still receiving oxygen from a mask, and then she'll be breathing all on her own, without a safety net. Everyone's in Cubicle 4, everyone's grinning and blinking away tears and looking at Renée.

When Tereza takes over the watch from me, early on the morning of Friday, 18 July, Renée has moved her head and frowned a little. The sounds of the P.I.C.U. – it's a busy night with hectic admissions, lots of talking and walking – must be getting through to her. She's receiving hardly any anaesthesia now. Angelique says patients tend to wake up very gradually from medically induced comas: these could be the first signs. She stands with me for minutes, in spite of the rush, but Renée is no longer frowning, no longer moving. I clearly saw it. Angelique says she believes me. I believe her.

Tereza's sleep is still lingering in our room. I imagine that the frown was not a random twitch of the nerves, but an indication of deep dissatisfaction. It must be a good omen. Who else has ever been born twice, both times with a frown? I can't sleep, I'm dog tired, but the caffeine from what must be five espressos seems to be bombarding my heart. Just as I decide to send Tereza a text message to ask if she's noticed any more signs, my phone rings. Tereza. She says: "Come. Now."

I run across the expanse of grass, jump over the tame rabbits. Tereza has her reasons for calling me, for saying just those two words. Using mobile phones in the P.I.C.U. isn't allowed. She went to the waiting room, selected my number, waited for it to connect and said, "Come. Now." Her extraordinary control is actually a sign of great excitement. She didn't know I was still awake, she knew a telephone call would scare the hell out of me, but she had no choice. She had to talk calmly to avoid giving me a heart attack. She had to get back to Renée quickly, she wanted to avoid me asking any questions, or her voice sending out the wrong signal. She sent me a spoken text message, afraid I wouldn't notice a normal one in time. When I reach Clinic 12, my head's no longer receiving any oxygen and my thought processes have stopped; my legs are using everything that's available.

It's a second or a two, maybe three, a generous estimate; time starts from the moment the edge of the curtain in Cubicle 4 parts to reveal a nurse's back – to be precise, the curve of a pert derrière in uniform, followed by straight shoulders above a hollow back, Angelique, a metre from the foot of the bed, I have no time to listen to what she's saying, how she says it, and to connect that to her face, which I see in profile, because my eyes, as I get closer, lock on to Dr De Jager deeper inside Cubicle 4, to the left of the bed, she looks ready to step in, she's extremely focused, says nothing, her right hand is in the pocket of her lab coat, moving, touching something in there, she could see me if she weren't concentrating so hard on looking at the bed, and where the silhouette of her white coat stops, Tereza's hip begins, her posture as she leans forward, the absence of her arms, which she's reaching out in the same direction as Dr De Jager's gaze, and Tereza's stance, in the artificial light, brighter than it usually is at this time of day, the shadows cast by the light on her sharp, Slavic features, and everything I can see, her awkward position, the light, the composition, reminds me of the severity of a biblical scene in the baroque era, a winner of the World Press Photo contest, category: daily life. As I censor myself, banning these thoughts from my mind, I see the focus of the attention: Renée, half upright, leaning on thick pillows, only a second has gone by and the next, full, second I look at her face, which appears to have no expression, it could

172

be the agonising moment just before her death, her little head drooping, battered, dazed, the yellowish colour of her skin, anxiously I try to see her eyes, to see if she can see anything, if she's looking, and then, finally, the third second arrives, the most beautiful second in forty years of Emiel Steegman, which begins with a stimulus in my little girl's brain, a stimulus that reaches the brain by way of the eye: there's someone else present, in the corner of the cubicle – I feel that I can follow the connection, the communication, and that makes it seem as if I have a presentiment of what's going to happen, or as if I've predicted it, an impossible déjà vu, as if, like God Himself, I'm commanding her with my divine powers to roll her head a little on the pillow, to look at me, to recognise me, weakly and, because of the paralysis, with just one half of her mouth, to smile mischievously at me and to raise her left arm from the sheet and hold it out to me . . .

For two hours we can't take our eyes off her, can't be dragged away from her bedside. At first Dr De Jager keeps us company, standing back, observing how Renée reacts, what she does and what she doesn't do. She's clearly still groggy from the days of anaesthesia, but even so, mentally, she seems to be all there. She recognises her Bear, but she also knows that the crocodile at the foot of her bed, a gift from friends, is an interloper; she doesn't want him anywhere near her. She seems to realise she's been away for a little while, she doesn't know where she went, she just knows she's back now, and in her excitement she pays no attention as yet to the paralysis running exactly down the middle of her face. I also have the impression that she's not even trying to speak, not that she's forgotten she was ever capable of speech, I don't think it's that, nor do I think the tube in her throat is preventing her from trying, she simply doesn't need any words yet, she can fall back on or is reminded of that period of her life, really not all that long ago, when she had to get by without words but was still able to make contact with relative ease. Those first few hours are filled with excitement and the joy of our reunion. We're together again after a long journey. We still haven't left the airport.

Two hours later, Renée slips into a peaceful sleep. She can see us, and she knows who we are; this doesn't answer all of the questions about the cognitive impact of the stroke and the trauma, but it's certainly a good start. It's helped to keep the panic under control. Dr De Jager has established that Renée is blinking her eyes nicely, both at the same time. She explains to us that not all the muscles in the two sides of the body are controlled by the opposite half of the brain. Blinking is something you do simultaneously, left and right. The control is situated in the right side of the brain, but many of the little muscles around the right eye are governed by the left side of the brain. That could have meant her right eyelid wouldn't shut completely.

Later we unexpectedly receive an answer to a far more important question. We've been to Tereza's mother's for breakfast and a shower and when we return to the P.I.C.U. we immediately realise something's going on. We see Deborah and Evelyne's heads peeping around the curtain of Cubicle 4, we hear excited whispers as we approach. Renée's awake and is sitting on Angelique's lap, who finished her shift a while ago. She smiles impishly at us, big, hollow eyes. The tube has been removed from her throat. Angelique firmly holds her up straight and hands her a glass of pink liquid: Fristi, a fruit yoghurt drink, the carton is on one of the nursing trolleys. Renée's arm is shaky, but she manages to bring the glass to her mouth and to pour in some Fristi. Renée closes her mouth and swallows it down. She swallows, without spilling any, without coughing. The applause from the nurses and Dr De Jager must have sounded more spontaneous the first time, but even so, applause is a sound that's rarely heard in the P.I.C.U. Renée can swallow. Some muscular functions aren't located on the right or the left, but in the middle, along the body's axis. They require both halves of the brain to work together. If one half breaks down, you have to wait and see what the other half will manage to do on its own. Renée can swallow, without coughing, the flap closes off her windpipe. She'll be spared a lifetime with a feeding tube.

Everyone is of course relieved, overjoyed, at this wonderful news, everyone wants to see her, but some members of the family are hit harder by the sight of Renée awake than by the comatose Renée, six days ago. For six days the situation was so abstract: the illuminated mother ship, M.R.I. scans, medical terminology, language in general – we've been talking for six days. Now that Renée's awake, language is superfluous: looking reveals everything to the observer. This is how it is. The meaning of a stroke has become flesh. This reunion is a painful farewell. I comfort my parents in the waiting room.

175

Saturday afternoon, exactly a week after I fetched Renée from her grandma's and took her to Amélie's birthday party, we drive down a tunnel to Clinic 6. Fear and excitement in Renée's dilated pupils. She's getting a room all to herself in the H.D.U., the high dependency unit, a ward between the intensive care and the ordinary wards, with a sofa bed for a parent. A new nurse, Trina, is steering the bed, we're walking, a fast pace; I'm holding tightly to the front of the frame, in case she needs help. A strip of wooden boards has been fixed to the tunnel wall in both directions, improvised buffers for the expensive beds. At some intersections there's a misty convex mirror on the wall. The low arch of the tunnel, in particular, clad with pale-yellow tiles, creates the impression that we're passing beneath the Iron Curtain, heading for freedom.

The room isn't exactly cheery. The H.D.U. is on the ground floor of Clinic 6 and, unlike the higher floors in the building, it has no outside view: corridors, stairwells, lift shafts, consultation rooms and doctors' offices enclose the ward. Frosted glass has been used throughout to lure in as much light as possible. A duck, a goldfish, a frog are painted in broad strokes; Renée isn't impressed, turns her head away. Tereza organises, cheerfully attempts to make the place a bit cosier, as if we've just arrived at a holiday home. After ten minutes, Renée's excitement at the presence of a television fades. The cartoon is too hectic for her, she falls asleep. It's the middle of the day, we're sitting on opposite sides of her bed; we hardly dare look at each other.

Around six, after Renée's chewed a bit on a sandwich and eaten a fruit yoghurt, I say goodbye. She puts her arm around my neck and squeezes with all her might, in a strange combination of love, teasing and pent-up aggression – I struggle to free myself. On my way to the multistorey car park, I walk past parked cars in a blue zone for disabled people with special parking permits. One by one, I check out the cars, most of them estate cars, with space for the wheelchair and room for loading and unloading the immobile passenger. The Citroën C4 Picasso and the S.E.A.T. Altea XL aren't ugly, aren't only designed with practicality in mind. I'm surprised to see that most of the drivers have permanently stuck the obvious parking permit to the windscreen so they can't tuck it away in the glove box when they leave the blue zone.

I enjoy the car ride, the movement, the speed, the landscape opening up around me. The music on the radio. It's a summery Saturday evening, people are getting ready for the high point of the week. I know there's nothing waiting for me at home. Even before I've parked the car in front of the house, I'll want to get back to the duck, the goldfish, the frog, to the aluminium cage. When I drive into the village, I take a short detour. Mieke's phoned a few times over the past week. She's very concerned about Renée. About us. She's not doing it explicitly or intentionally, but she's looking for forgiveness; she feels, is convinced, that she did the wrong thing. I keep telling her she's not to blame. She gauges my voice when I talk about Renée. Just saying the words doesn't count: she needs to be able to hear it for herself, in my voice. If she can hear that I mean it, that's

177

a kind of forgiveness. Because of course I can't actually forgive her. Forgiving her would, after all, imply guilt. Mieke is innocent; Renée is my daughter. And yet I take a detour, I avoid Mieke, Paul and Amélie's house, at the top of my street. I don't want to see that they're at home, or that they're out somewhere.

Lodewijk's mowing his front lawn. As soon as he sees me, he starts walking towards me with his ponderous gait. He's angry when the vague rumour he's heard turns out to be true. He shakes his head, looking down at the ground, outraged by so much injustice, furious. One foot in front of the other, his hands on his hips.

I feel like a stranger in my own house. It's the house of before Saturday, 12 July. I try to numb myself with triviality, a game show, sausages with ketchup, news about the Tour, female nude, homeopathic remedies and bottles of beer. I kick off my shoes, play the carefree bachelor. Just after midnight, I wake up on the two-seater sofa, there's noise outside, the muffled thumping of a beat, not too far away. Young people partying in a marquee, the noise blows across the house in waves. One day Renée will want to go. I push her wheelchair through the trampled grass and mud to some stinking party. Perhaps I'll need some help to get my little girl onto the wooden floor as it bounces up and down with all those pogoing louts, won't be able to do it by myself. I heave myself up off the sofa, go upstairs, to her room, fall onto the canopy bed. Her pillow: the scent hits me in the gut. It's the scent of before, of safe, of the unspoken future with a good degree and a decent husband. Should I hope she falls for a woman? A gentle, caring, sweet woman? Should I pray she doesn't stoop to a man who was never intended for her beauty, who resents her for his own simmering shame, showing it at first with silence, then with words, then finally with his fists, easy prey, just as in the beginning? – I'll murder him. I swear it.

It's nothing to do with me, I think, as if I'm not the one who's sitting at the wheel and operating the pedals. I drive past the turn-off for the hospital and head for the city centre. I park underground. Sunday morning, early, people on the street, fresh bread the only thing on their minds. Twice I walk along the Glass Street, I act as if I'm taking the shortest route somewhere. Nearly all the curtains are closed. The occasional empty bar stool, but with no neon light. I walk around the block, don't really know what I'm looking for, what I hope to see. I saunter along the narrow side streets, where there are more windows. I remember our trip to Portugal, the mountains along the Douro, a fox walking by, just a couple of metres away, because I was sitting so quietly in my spot in the woods. After ten minutes leaning against a wall with my phone to my ear, I return to the car.

Back above ground, as I drive into the street, I catch a glimpse of a woman disappearing around the corner; the one-way system forces me in the other direction. It can't have been. Perhaps I'm not seeing her, but recognising her in another woman. If it wasn't Sandra, which I assume it wasn't, then it certainly could have been her. Her posture, height, long hair, prominent bosom. A small leopard-print handbag.

Renée's in a bad mood. She hits us, her lower jaw jutting angrily. Tereza and I are perplexed. What are we supposed to do? Her rage is understandable, and how else can she express it? She makes no attempts to speak. Not a sign on her face, not a movement of her mouth, nothing in her eyes to indicate that a word is on its way. Her control system has completely gone. Does she still think in language? How desperate must she feel when she hears Tereza and me talking, about her? When we speak to her? Asking her a question in a futile attempt to find out how we can help her, what she wants? Is there a cacophony of sentences echoing around inside her head, searching for her vocal cords, or is it unbearably quiet in there? We can't allow her to hit us, can't let it become normal. Whenever we calmly try to explain this to her, she cries and wants a hug.

A child psychologist comes to see us. Nathalie. She's in charge of the psychotherapy element of the rehabilitation programme that will begin in a few days. She's made a card for Renée, a laminated A4 with various symbols on it: a glass of water, a plate and cutlery, a bed, an unhappy face, a potty with a roll of toilet paper beside it. Renée isn't impressed, doesn't join in, doesn't point at anything. Frustration is the first major hurdle, says Nathalie in the corridor. We need to give her some time. It's an advantage that Renée's so young. She hardly ever sees actual depression in young children after severe traumas with serious physical conse-quences. Which is generally the case with adults. Children of that age don't think for too long about the future or the past. She asks if I have a camcorder. Video recordings could

180

help her later, when she's a bit older, to process what happened, to put things in place, to close a chapter.

In front of the H.D.U.'s secure entrance, at the point where the hallway along the length of Clinic 6 meets the narrower corridors to the adjacent outpatients' clinic, a small sitting area has been set up. The slim, low armchairs in brown faux leather have tapered legs, the tables, two of them, have a black lacquered surface with a Japanese-looking flower design. It looks as if it's been plucked straight from some hip vintage store, but these pieces of furniture are new, you can smell it. There's a drinks machine too, hot drinks. The chocolate milk's made with water. That flavour. I'm ten years old: chlorine, wet hair, sugary waffle.

I receive a panicky phone call. Renée has a headache. I run to her room. Twice now she's pointed at her head, at exactly the site of her stroke. Woken from an afternoon nap, crying with pain. She gets a big dose of painkillers, the doctors stay nearby. We cancel the visitors. She can't lie still, she can't rest. Again we endure an eternity, this one forty minutes long. Then her pulse rate slows. Her head has sunk deep into the pillow, her eyes go from left to right, from Mummy to Daddy. A sigh, a smile, her index finger raised questioningly towards the T.V.

I sit beside Renée on the bed, she leans into my arm and we watch Knofje. No idea – as I can see through the window beneath the television, the way the doctors are talking to Tereza: they just don't know. I don't need to hear what they're saying. Wait. Observe. Knofje's a little girl with red hair. Trina brought the D.V.D. in; her daughter's mad about Knofje. I imagine it, in the evening after her shift, her daughter the same age as ours, the realisation. She tells her about a sweet little girl who's very poorly, about Renée, enticing her to offer her D.V.D. of her own accord. Knofje will cheer up Renée. Short films about a quirky little girl. Surreal, brightly coloured sets. That's how Knofje sees the house where she lives, this is how she experiences the world. I feel jealous for Renée and also for myself. A clear and colourful life full of small events. After a few episodes it starts to feel as if the Renée we've lost has merged with Knofje, and I can no longer watch.

My first night at the H.D.U. Tereza's sleeping at her mother's, she only gets scared in our house. It's warm in the room, beads of sweat form in the downy hairs on Renée's top lip. She's wearing a vest, nothing else. She's lying on a quilt, which I replace after hearing a quiet trickle. In the middle of the night, I climb into bed with her. I hug her and look at her face from close up. A perfect landscape. Will I have enough love? Will I be able to keep pulling her up out of the depths, again and again? What's happened to the strength that should keep such agonising questions at bay?

Renée wakes up calm. Cheerful. She smiles at her daddy, close beside her in the hospital bed. The early morning sunlight pierces the frosted glass. She stretches lazily, a cat, her skin soft and gleaming like fur. It's July 21, Belgium's national holiday, and it looks as if it's going to be a big day for Renée. Because of yesterday's headache, lots of visitors are coming this afternoon. If Renée can't handle it and she kicks up a fuss, then so be it. Everyone has to understand that she gets tired quickly. Tereza and I can't guarantee anything. I plan to drift along calmly on the tide of the day.

Tereza looks radiant; Renée's breakfast hasn't been ordered yet. I know Tereza has forced herself not to come an hour earlier. She greets us with a surprise, a possibility that Nathalie had mentioned yesterday. A wheelchair. Not an ordinary wheelchair: a red one. It has small, thick tyres, and the seat is a layer of foam, sealed inside gleaming red plastic and moulded to fit the body of a seated child. Safety belts as in a Formula 1 racing car.

We go for a ride around Clinic 6. Renée is all eyes. I slowly push her along the corridors, so she gets an idea of the size of the paediatric ward and understands that she's in the company of lots of other sick children. After lunch, it's time: the first trip outside. Fresh air. We decide to gather the visitors at a table outside a cafeteria in the main building. Renée welcomes grandmas and grandpas, aunts and uncles with a big hug, everyone's delighted to see her in the wheelchair, out of her bed. Tereza's mum's partner, Renée's "Uncle Luk" – the two of them are as thick as thieves – buys her a Cornetto. Her first ice cream, a milestone; from now on, an ice cream every day for Miss Renée! Glasses clinking, laughter, and while Renée presses the cone to her mouth and then licks her lips clean, an unusual technique, the Tour de France and the political impasse are discussed, and our misfortune briefly fades into the background.

*

In the early evening I walk with Renée around the green
space between the clinics. She's slept for an hour or so. The
day's too nice to stay in the room. It's peaceful, the visitors
have withdrawn and dispersed beyond the traffic barrier. I
make quick, crazy swerves, in and out of the ground floor
of the multistorey car park. I hear Renée laughing, the
sound of her glee amplified by the half-empty space. I push
her deeper into the building and give a quick shout, so she
can hear the echo. Then, suddenly, she lets out a yell and
listens to its repeat. She shouts, it hardly seems to surprise
her, this deliberate sound that's coming from her throat.
Crying, laughing, and now shouting, too. It sounds normal,
like before, I recognise her voice in it. We both shout and
pay no attention to the people and their curious glances.
There's no variation, the volume is all she can control. She
shouts it all out, until she's red in the face, and then she
laughs. I call Tereza, let her hear it.

A green dress with short sleeves, big watery eyes and a
boy's haircut. Dr Joke De Hoorne comes into our life. Into
our room. She's the children's rheumatologist and she's
brought Trina with her, who'll look after Renée while we
have a talk. While she talks to us. In a room in the H.D.U.
that we've never been invited to enter before. Room: four
tables lined up in the middle. Dr De Hoorne on one side, us
on the other. Rheumatologist. I think about Renée's joints,
wonder what's wrong with them. The doctor begins by
skimming through a summary of the past ten days: patient
Renée Steegman, constantly glancing up as if asking for
confirmation, as if we can still change the report now, but
this is our last chance. When the summary's over, she rests

one elbow on the edge of the table. First she supports her chin, then she takes hold of her neck. All the doctors, she says, all the relevant specialists from the children's ward had a meeting this afternoon. As research into the cause of the inflammation of the blood vessel hasn't found anything, they can't entirely rule out the possibility of a congenital weakness. It's a very slim chance, overshadowed by the more obvious explanation: a defect in her immune system. If there's no trace of intruders, then the body itself must have caused the inflammation. The white blood cells have become overactive, they started to fight against an invisible – sorry, I mean non-existent – enemy, but there was actually nothing wrong. In some children, this causes inflammation of the joints and they get rheumatism. In Renée's case, it was in the brain. This diagnosis, says Dr De Hoorne, an auto-immune disease, obviously has consequences for Renée. She holds her head at a slight angle, her eyes showing and asking for understanding, she wishes she could tell us something else. Renée will have a course of chemotherapy and cortisone treatment for at least a year. The chemo is intended to reprogram her white blood cells. Her defences need to be knocked down and rebuilt from scratch, in the hope that the white blood cells will behave normally after that.

In the hope that?
  Yes.
  And what if it doesn't work?
  If it doesn't work, it could happen again.
  An inflammation?
  Yes, an inflammation.

185

Do you mean a stroke?

The cortisone will do a lot to protect her for the first year, and of course we'll monitor her condition with regular M.R.I. scans . . .

Do you mean she could have another stroke?

Yes, it's possible. In the other half of the brain . . .

When?

Tension in the green fabric as her shoulders reach their highest point, just before the abrupt drop: could be tomorrow, could be fifteen years. We're assuming the treatment will work.

And then, tomorrow, or in fifteen years, what then?

Just the tension in the fabric, which lasts a long time, before slowly subsiding. Dr De Hoorne doesn't say it out loud, but the message is clear. Another stroke and it'll all be over.

I'm sitting in one of the brown faux-leather chairs. There must be a secret route, different from the tunnels, that starts somewhere around here, near the drinks machine, at this deserted intersection of time and space. I should take a closer look. I stand up and walk around, Dr De Hoorne's words haunting me, the verdict. Sometimes I see men, fathers, they smoke a cigarette in the courtyard, drink a coffee, I never see any of them again. How can that be? I look, run my hands around doorframes, press a switch or two. I'm missing something. Back in the armchair, I notice a mark on the side of the drinks machine. The paint's gone, the metal's visible. A man approaches, a father. He rummages around in both pockets, but doesn't take anything out. No cigarettes, no coins, no mobile. He saunters around the machine, keeping an eye on me, maybe he knows about it, someone's tipped him off about this escape route and he's about to discover the mark on the side of the machine. Maybe it can only happen once. Instantaneously. A parallel world with the same people, different. He makes a mistake, he leaves a little space, I appear beside him. I look him squarely in the face, and I see it, his fear, I've beaten him to it. As I press myself against the machine, blocking the way for his arm to make a last-ditch attempt, my right hand groping around the side, I feel where the smooth gloss paint ends, and I touch the mark.

THREE

THREE

I

His first name's Paul; I've forgotten his surname. He's wearing a white polo shirt and baggy blue trousers. The physiotherapy room is flooded with sunlight. Equipment and colourful props are stacked in one corner, the walls have those wooden bars on them that make gyms all over the world look the same, and have done so for a few hundred years. A balding fifty-something with boundless enthusiasm, kneeling on a thick mat. Renée sits between his legs, on her heels, her back towards him. His arm around her chest holds her as if in a harness. She looks sweaty, dazed from the exertion, not interested in whatever it is that Paul's planning to do with her next.

I hear Valeria and tap the pause button. Willem's been in bed for an hour or two already and he'll sleep right through until morning. My office is next to our bedroom; I listen, wait for the click of the switch that turns off her lamp. I put headphones on.

I have shown inhuman levels of patience – and not by choice. Four days after the sad news, two days before the funeral, three video cassettes the size of Tic Tac boxes are lying on the dining table until well after noon, next to the envelope they came in that morning, which has carefully been sliced open. Name of sender: Emiel Steegman. It's his handwriting: the ink is from a fountain pen.

Felix was in the editing studio and couldn't get away immediately. Luckily he recognised the cassettes as soon as he saw them. He collects old stuff: turntables, analogue cameras, vintage toasters, table lamps, wristwatches and ties, as well as telex machines and early personal computers. Typewriters. I got the same model from him as the one Steegman presumably wrote *T* on, an Olympia S.G.1. At least that's the typewriter that's mentioned in the book. Schreibmaschine Gross 1. Manufactured in the late 1950s, in Wilhelmshaven. I once used it to type a few initial attempts at the biography. It felt wrong. Beautiful shoes, the right size, moulded to a stranger's feet. And, of course, it's such a hassle.

Felix was sure to have the matching camcorder, and a firewire cable somewhere too; the tricky thing would be finding a computer with a suitable port. Half an hour ago I received a file with the name "E.S.".

In the motionless image, inside the room that's illuminating my little office, the beginning of an action. Paul is leaning forward, his chest touching the back of Renée's head.

It surprised me at first, but less so as time went on, the way Steegman wrote nothing about his daughter, about her stroke and the uncertainty that followed. She does admittedly play an important role in *T*, published two years later, but until the end of the story she remains younger than the age at which it actually happened to her. And after *T*, after all that insanity, he made nothing else public.

Paul pushes her – an abrupt manoeuvre, unannounced. Together they fall forward onto the mat, he braces with one arm and catches her with the other, she hangs in the harness. He praises her, says she's doing great, that she can have a rest now. He nods at the camera: Did you see that? I hear Steegman, it must be his voice that says, "Yes." The shoulder, says Paul, start with the shoulder, then the upper arm, always build up slowly from the torso. He praises Renée again, she's worked hard, and he carries her to a bright-red wheelchair.

What are they talking about?

I watch the fall a second time, in slow motion. His upper body forces her forward. The arm around her chest is also holding onto her left arm. With his left arm he prevents them both from smacking into the mat – she's unable to use her left arm, and her right arm dangles limply.

After the third time, I understand: he's trying to trigger a reflex reaction. It's brilliant! He's appealing to her instincts. It's impossible for her to move her free right arm deliberately, Renée isn't capable, but in an emergency, when gravity threatens to slam her to the mat, the body has to intervene to protect itself and the brain intuitively finds a path to the one arm that can save her: a new, rerouted connection, which so far has reached her shoulder. That route has to be expanded now, extended deep into her arm.

I recognise this corridor. I can hear the clicking footsteps of Steegman, or perhaps Tereza. Judging by the length of the steps: Steegman. This corridor runs down the middle of the children's rehabilitation centre at the university hospital. I've only been there twice. The first time, Dr Van Der Linden, the consultant, wasn't there. I walked to the end of the corridor and back. On the wall were photographs of children who'd been treated there. I took photos of the photos and discovered only later that Renée was one of the children, unrecognisably swollen up because of the cortisone. A "moonface". Her round head in a witch's hat has been snipped from a photo and is part of a collage that she probably made herself. Bits of black paper, aluminium foil, stars and a glued-on drinking straw with a feather on the end as a magic wand. A spider drawn on one cheek, with its web on the other. Halloween.

At a rough estimate, it took me a year to reconstruct exactly what happened to Renée. Dr Van Der Linden spoke to me, friendly yet suspicious, about the consequences of a non-congenital brain injury, until I dropped the name "Steegman", a brick, from a great height, onto the middle of her desk, at which point she showed me the door, still friendly, but brisk. Her reaction, she said, had nothing to do with his celebrity, there are no degrees to the confidentiality of a medical file. A modest, intelligent woman, dedicated to the rehabilitation centre. And me, a naughty boy, caught out.

The sound of singing slips in between the footsteps, two voices, at the bottom of the picture Steegman's hand takes hold of a handle and slowly opens a door. A small room, Renée sits at a table beside Gaby, Gabriële, the speech therapist. They act as if they haven't noticed Steegman coming in, although they're facing the door. Renée focuses her attention on a big cassette recorder inside a black faux-leather case with holes for the buttons and the speaker, through which a voice is coming, which she tries to follow with her own. Gaby watches, satisfied, and almost inaudibly joins in with the wordless song.

This is the scene Steegman was aiming to present. Excited by this demonstration of a remarkable breakthrough, he's raced to the room for his camcorder. Like a film director, he decides to incorporate the element of surprise into the film: walking along the corridor, up to the door behind which his daughter turns out to be using singing exercises to regain control of her voice.

After a while Renée stops, suddenly embarrassed by all the fuss. She casts a furtive glance at the camera. Then her chin sinks to her chest and her smile becomes a grimace; still in her wheelchair she sinks into Gaby's lap, sobbing.

The next clip is barely four seconds long.

The frame is filled with a large white pillow against the headboard of her bed. Renée is leaning into the feathers at a slight angle. It's early, she's wearing a sleeveless nightdress, maybe the curtains are still closed; the picture's grainy somehow, as if it's twilight in the room. Her right hand's lying, wrist bent, on the edge of her tray, next to a carton of chocolate milk and a plate with half a slice of bread on it. Renée's holding up the other half to her messy mouth. She's looking down.

As soon as I start the clip, the girl looks straight into the lens. It grabs me by the throat. She's crying, but it's different from in the previous clip. This isn't sadness or self-pity welling up, she's not being ambushed and robbed of her breath – she takes a bite of the bread, chews. The question on her helpless little face is almost audible: what

I am doing here, Daddy? With an awareness too adult for a small child, she looks away, without any reproach, alone with her silent desperation and a slice of bread in the hollow of a thick pillow.

He puts down the camcorder, of course; he slides onto the high bed beside her, one foot on the floor. He decides to say nothing, any attempts to comfort her will only fuel the sadness, make it flare up again, he even ensures that he barely touches her. He feels awful about each and every one of the four seconds he filmed her, and yet in a strange way he's pleased to have captured this elusive emotion. The pure pitch-black beauty of it.

I can still smell the holiday home, the hint of sauerkraut that the heat of the radiators or the sun made the brown curtains give off. Luckily it was already nice and warm during the daytime on Cap Gris-Nez, so we didn't spend much time indoors. The holiday was a present for my thirtieth birthday, from my parents and brother; it had been at least ten years since we'd last spent more than a weekend under the same roof. I wasn't expecting any other gifts, but at breakfast that fateful day a bottle of Veuve Clicquot appeared, along with a beautiful edition of a brand-new translation of *Moby-Dick*, and *The Murderer*.

I'd heard of Emiel Steegman but not read anything by him. He seemed too serious for his own good, a writer grumpily tripping himself up as he carries the weight of world literature on his shoulders like a cast-iron globe. How I'd reached that conclusion: no idea. An awkward interview on the radio, an author's photo, an editor's comment overheard. Not much, not much at all. Exactly the kind of thing he'd condemn in *T*.

By the time I closed the book, I'd missed two meals. I wasn't hungry. The beach was empty, the tide was out, the bay between Cap Gris-Nez and Cap Blanc-Nez had been transformed into a sandy plain that must be visible from space. I got up and started walking. I closed my eyes. I knew there was nothing to bump into, not for miles. The high wind blowing across the North Sea roared in my ears. I resisted the temptation to open my eyes after a while, and the urge didn't return. Everything disappeared. I forgot about the beach, I forgot about my legs and I forgot about the wind. For the second time on my birthday I vanished from the face of the earth, away from the shabby show that was my life.

Crime and Punishment. Dostoevsky. The comparison couldn't be missed: on the first page of *The Murderer*, Ferdinand, a mild-mannered widower of seventy-three, splits open his young neighbour's skull with a hatchet. No-one accused Steegman of imitating the greats. He was the *new* Dostoevsky, a Dostoevsky for the twenty-first century, more intense, more inventive. No-one had expected another writer like that to come along, everyone was pleasantly surprised.

It was only with *T* that Steegman really became Steegman. No-one compared him to another writer. *He* was now the benchmark.

Ironically, six months later, that was the nail the Volckaert family's lawyer kept hammering away at. Steegman's position and influence brought with them certain moral obligations, which he had sorely neglected in this book. On the third day of the trial I sat near the lawyer, Pieters, and could see the pleasure the man took in every opportunity to think himself superior to this author who'd had such a great success. The way he stretched his back, puffed up his chest and looked down his nose at the accused's camp. Sandra's brother, a little hooligan with a tattoo on his neck, stared impassively ahead, her mother sank deeper into her seat every time her daughter's name was mentioned.

In a poetic passage in the first part of the book, the famous writer T envisages all the small, innocent misunderstandings, half-truths and loose interpretations that, via biographers and secondary literature, have unobtrusively found their way into the collective consciousness. He mentally gathers the books in a large town square, huge piles, tightly packed together, a terrifying edifice with narrow corridors, no more than slits between towering walls, through which the public shuffles along sideways, desperately looking for an exit. A scene, he thinks, that Stanley Kubrick would have known what to do with. I read the book in the same spot as I read *The Murderer*. November, this time, the end of November, the sun so low that every irregularity on the sandy plain is revealed by a shadow, and mine stretched out into the dunes, appeared to be rising up into the air.

My head was fizzing like a glass of lemonade. This philosophical thriller, or existential detective novel, or however the book came to be described afterwards, was, to me, nothing less than a glorious provocation.

Just like *The Murderer*, *T* is built around a relatively simple idea, a brainwave – the centre of gravity around which the novel keeps its balance, no matter what flights of fancy the story takes, and so remains believable. T, prompted by his daughter of almost four, develops a "bio-phobia", a fear of his own biography, the only book with his name on the cover over which he has absolutely no control. The fear of losing his life after his death: that's what it says in the blurb for the first edition. He carries out an investigation, effectively incognito, disguised as himself, to find out who he is in the eyes of other people, what stories and impressions will take root, what kind of father his daughter will have if he drops down dead in the street tomorrow.

A crucifixion. Two Danish reviewers and *The New York Review of Books* were the first to see the "T" as, undoubt-edly, the Tau Cross, a grim prefiguration of what, according to Steegman, is awaiting T. What is awaiting himself. A crucifixion, after his death, a public execution, mis-understood like Jesus Christ. Others saw the absence of the missing top section of the cross as an intellectual decapitation.

What is interesting, and not without significance in a story such as this, is that Steegman based much of the novel on his own life, as he became overwhelmed by sudden fame. T's decision to stop talking about his work in mid-interview, in mid-sentence, followed by the exhaus-tive analyses of those last words, is of course a direct allusion to what happened to Steegman himself after the aborted interview on the T.V. news on the evening of his historic win, the Golden Belly Band, his last public appearance. But also: Tereza, his wife, Renée, his daughter, the house, his parents, childhood friends. Steegman was playing a high-stakes game with reality. The stake? Evading a biography, perhaps that, too. You could compare the book to one of those stingers that the police roll out across road surfaces to bring fleeing criminals to a stop.

For me, his brilliant literary scare tactics had achieved the opposite effect. The louder his voice resounded from the book, assuring me there was nothing else to find, not one single scrap, that he'd used everything that was important in his novel, that my attempts would never achieve any semblance of validity and were doomed to founder in the quicksand of my assumptions, the more interesting the idea of being his biographer began to seem.

Banana-yellow flags hang across the ceiling from corner to corner. A narrow room on the third floor of Clinic 6; chemotherapy. Eight years after my decision, a week after my fortieth birthday, I watch video images sent to me by the man who vanished into thin air. I look through his eyes. I see what he saw. He has a good reason for doing this. There's a reason for this eccentric behaviour. Is he still trying to cast his own light on events? How else am I to explain this direct communication? It would certainly be a very strange way of trying to pull yet more wool over my eyes.

I have to pay attention, I mustn't get distracted. I feel that I should be peering into the corners, exploring the edges. It'll appear somewhere in the picture, just by chance, briefly, over in a flash, something that, after some pondering and puzzling, will challenge everything that is known about the circumstances surrounding Sandra Volckaert's death.

It's not really a room, the walls aren't made of brick.

A glass cubicle, Renée is sitting on a high bed facing the window, the toxic Endoxan trickling into her body through a drip. Then she has to be flushed out twenty-four hours later to prevent damage to her liver and kidneys.

Steegman's shadow falls diagonally across her legs. For something to say, or as part of the commentary for the video he's recording, he asks who's coming to visit her. The camera pans right, zooming in on a small delegation approaching along the decorated corridor. A woman, a photographer, or someone who has taken it upon herself to take photos, comes in, says hello and asks if she can stand next to Steegman. She's followed by the head of the department and a slight man in a T-shirt, with a timid smile on his face. Tereza's there too, off screen, the man shakes her hand first; congratulations are offered in English. Then, after a glance into the lens, he says hello to Steegman, who replies: Congratulations on your win. The man holds out his hand to Renée, smiles like one child recognising another. Steegman asks if she's going to shake his hand, the gentleman's come all the way from Spain. From Spain, repeats Tereza with feigned amazement. Renée smiles and holds out her left hand, the photographer asks her to look at the birdie.

Carlos Sastre. It must be the Tuesday after the Tour de France reached Paris. Yesterday he raced the lucrative criterium in Uigem, nearby; today he's showing his charitable side.

The photographer has a problem with her camera; she asks them to give her just one tiny moment, and Carlos Sastre and Renée Steegman freeze in their handshake like two seasoned world leaders. When it's done, Renée

201

receives a signed photograph and a gentle touch on the cheek. As if she didn't see anything, Tereza says even before the delegation has left the room: What have you got there? Did the nice man give you something?

Hair loss will be minimal. The course of treatment is not designed to combat cancer. Her reduced immunity means avoiding public spaces as much as possible. Swimming pools, indoor playgrounds, public transport. A cold could prove fatal.

It's her fourth birthday, 10 August, 2008. Her hair hangs down beneath her snug party hat, thin and straight, shoulder-length. She's sitting at the head of the table, which is covered with pink paper. The cortisone and the associated increase in appetite can already be seen in her cheeks. She takes her right arm by the wrist and arranges it neatly beside her cardboard plate, which has a Disney princess on it. She's sitting in an ordinary children's chair, without the custom-made support to compensate for the imbalance in her back. Nice and straight, her muscles strong.

Although only Renée is in the frame, I can hear a low murmur of noise from visitors who have just arrived. They're at home, through the window I recognise the yew hedge that screens off the garden from the narrow path leading to Schoolstraat. Over her shoulder, through the corner window of the living room, I can see François Moens's house across the road.

It was the strangest feeling to be sitting in the sun-room that is described so precisely in T – the first of many strange experiences. By pure coincidence, I spoke to François Moens first, shortly after the book came out. I just wanted to see the street, the neighbourhood, maybe catch a glimpse of Steegman. In front of the house was a large, modern advertising board: FOR SALE. TWO STYLISH HOMES IN A COUNTRY SETTING. Mr Moens was standing by the gutter, hosing out his green wheelie bin for garden waste. As I drove past, he turned to the road and gave me a long hard stare. He was wearing a white vest and red jogging bottoms, pulled up high. In the sunroom he repeated his answer, his rhetorical question, several times: Why are you asking *me* about it? Leaning forward in his armchair, pointing at himself with both hands on his chest, a cynical twist to his smile; that book has left a sour taste in his mouth. He said his wife, Arlette, had died eight months ago. He raised his chin as he spoke her name, a man who is staying strong, nobly rising above his grief. Her flowery apron wasn't hanging on that single hook on the white wall. I thought, given the hospitable welcome I'd received in the sunroom, it would be inappropriate even to consider the thought that his wife might have been laid to rest in her apron.

Renée receives her gifts. A princess dress with puffed sleeves and tulle hangs on an armchair behind her. The visitors remain off screen, everyone is wary, the interaction with the birthday girl is awkward and overenthusiastic. Tereza helps to tear open an envelope, Steegman is also very interested in what's inside: a button or a shell on a string, apparently a good-luck charm, made by her best friend, Luna, the daughter of poet Xander Nevski and his wife Lena. Nevski is her surname; he was born with the names Van Nieuwenhuyze and Alexander. Luna remains standing beside Renée, gives her a helping hand. More oohs and aahs as the parcels are opened. They speak quietly, they're expecting silence. Her silence.

She blows out the candles on the Winnie-the-Pooh cake in two goes. Happy birthday to her. Happy birthday, dear Renée.

Luna and Renée sit beside each other on one chair. They eat pieces of cake from the same plate. Renée has taken off her birthday hat. The line at the front of her skull is covered with a layer of down. Nevski is in shot, he's holding a wide glass of Trappist beer up to his mouth. Next to his head: the white house where Mrs Schouteet, the widow in *T*, lives. I complimented her on her spacious living room, which opened onto three flowery patios. Facing in three directions. She was a sun worshipper, she laughed. Always had been. Three times she said: Vicky? No . . . I was tempted to try another name. It was as if she were inviting me to do so. Not Vicky, no. But I'd have to work out for myself who it actually was.

François Moens reacted only with bewilderment when I rather timidly mentioned the girl's name. He looked at me, not even quizzically, a strange, empty gaze in which I thought I detected signs of Alzheimer's. Convinced that Vicky had been a figment of Steegman's imagination, the beginning of an aborted storyline, the suggestion of a crime, inspired by the ridiculously low price of his house, the unoccupied place next door and Arlette and François' unfulfilled wish for a child, with no other aim than creating tension early on in the story, I went for coffee with Lodewijk Wesselmans and his wife, who lived across the road. Vicky caused a slight hiccup in the conversation. Lodewijk cast a stealthy glance at his wife, who stoically stirred her mint tea and said: We wouldn't know anything about that.

A family of bakers? The manager of the estate agent's didn't pay any attention to the owners of the houses he sold. He was interested only in the properties. His explanation? People from the city want to renovate farmhouses, locals want to build.

In the front room, on a white deep-pile rug, Luna and Renée pose for the camera. They're dressed up, Luna's wearing a traditional flamenco dress, Renée's in the princess dress that was just hanging on the armchair in the living room. They're standing next to each other, shoulder to shoulder. Renée is held upright by Tereza, behind her, and Julie, Tereza's sister, at the front of the picture. Everyone's excited; cries of admiration, of encouragement accompany the scene. Luna's hands and arms appear, she's making a video with her camera. Renée effectively hides herself by looking directly at Luna instead. She smiles with her lopsided mouth.

He can't help recording the image. It's a celebration, a happy sight, of course. He keeps a close eye on her. Who came up with the idea of holding her up on both legs? Is that a good idea? Good for whom? Isn't this display, naturally with the best of intentions, staged for everyone who finds it difficult to see Renée like that? What about the girl who'll have to sit down again soon?

Her resemblance to Tereza struck me when I arrived at the brasserie. Flushed from all the activity, Julie came quickly through the tables towards me, a smile on her face, arms outstretched to take my coat. After the sole meunière and the tarte Tatin, I waited for another hour or two. I didn't drink any alcohol, wrote in a notebook, read a magazine. When I spoke to her, she would know I wasn't a drunken idiot, but a man to be taken seriously. How badly I'd tripped up over that even-tempered smile as she moved among her customers, always available.

Those first few weeks I made a lot of mistakes, misjudging or approaching people in the wrong way more than once. It didn't take me long to work out that writing the biography of a living author, one who was a success, was not going to be an easy task. Luckily I was able to do a lot of research before the trial and the media furore began. It became even more difficult afterwards. Sometimes I pretended I was a novelist just to obtain certain information. "Novelist" was more effective than "journalist" or "biographer".

Early in the book, when T's head is reeling at the thought of everything that might have an influence on his biography, he divides us into three categories. The fan, the academic and the opportunist. He wonders which biographer he has most to fear from. The fanatical academic who seizes the opportunity to make a name for himself by piggybacking on his fame. But worst of all: the ones who are determined to explain his work. The ones who don't want to believe that he made it all up.

Soon after that, the story shifts in another direction. A hilarious scene at a school reunion with a steamy dance party is the first in a series of encounters featuring absurd dialogues and mutual misunderstandings, as T, still rather patiently and calmly, tries to make minor adjustments to people's perception of anecdotes from the past. Occasionally it seems as if, cutting straight across people and time, he is addressing his biographer directly, dictating passages of his book.

Through the glass door in the hallway that separates the front room from the living room at the back, Steegman films the sofa, where Tereza and Renée are lying together and looking down past their feet at the T.V. It must be early evening. I can't see the television. I think I recognise the music, fairy tale; something magical is happening. Then I hear the fairy, who's just appeared in a shining circle of light, and says to the sleeping Geppetto that he's given so much joy to others that he deserves for his own wish to come true. She brings Pinocchio to life. Tereza is turned on her side, with her knees slightly pulled up, enclosing Renée against the back cushions of the sofa. Steegman zooms in on their faces. Tereza blinks only occasionally, Renée hardly at all. Serene, calm, mother and child. A "stolen" image, which he deems valuable, this brief moment of nothing and yet everything.

In the garden, visitors, Renée is sitting with Luna and her little brother Ramon on a blue picnic blanket that's spread out on the grass. They're wearing hats to protect them from the sun. Lots of toys lying around, they've been playing for a while. A plane passes overhead, high and slow, the sound falling listlessly from the sky.

They've decided to let the girls play together regularly, as often as possible. It's good for both of them and very important for Renée. They live quite far apart, but it's summer and the holidays.

As I try to take everything in and to place it all, the

trees and bushes, the hedge, the path, a peculiar but definite "no" suddenly rings out. It comes from her mouth. It doesn't seem to startle Steegman, no-one reacts. More "no"s follow, even when something else is meant, even "yes". Everything is "no".

The atmosphere is not the same as at the birthday party. They understand that it's better for the girl not to be the centre of attention all the time. Her magnetic silence has been abandoned, with a simple "no" – she can, albeit in a limited way, express herself, make herself heard. They want her to feel that she's a child like any other, like Luna and Ramon.

But of course she's not like any other child. Steegman keeps her in shot when she finally remains alone on the blanket. Luna and Ramon run around, whooping, disappear into the house, return to their parents' table with a children's tea set on a tray, blissfully unaware. Giggling, they ask who wants coffee and who wants tea. One euro. Nevski asks them if they're con merchants and just serving up water. No, no, they're not. Lovely coffee. Espresso!

Holding the camera out in front of him, he searches for Tereza's face. She's noticed too, nods, suggests Luna and Ramon should go and drink coffee with Renée now. Steegman can't stand it any longer. He runs to his daughter, who's puffing and snorting and angrily pointing at the table. He asks what's that she's got there, and she looks over her shoulder at an ice bucket, filled with water. There's a frog floating in it. Her face lights up, she turns around and pushes the frog under. Excited by the prospect of fun, she makes her way towards him, first by dragging her weight sideways across the ground and then, drawing herself upright, she walks on her knees. Concentrating, she takes minuscule steps to the edge of the blanket. In the middle of his question about what she's planning to do, she aims the plastic frog at the camera and squeezes a spurting jet of water out of it . . . .

Steegman walks slowly, watching what he's recording on the display, through the house to the front room, where Renée's made a kind of throne out of cushions. From her elevated position, she's watching T.V. He kneels on the white rug, so the camera is at the same height as her face. She pays no attention to him. Look angry, he whispers after a while, and Renée presses her lips together until there's hardly any colour or mouth remaining. Her expression is ice cold, scary, and immune to Steegman's pent-up laughter. He zooms in on her eyes and whispers: smile. A huge grin pushes her chubby cheeks upwards. She flutters her eyelashes coquettishly. The game continues until a children's song comes on the T.V. There's a dance beat to it. Automatically Renée starts enthusiastically moving her shoulders, turning her head this way and that, she's sitting but she's dancing. He thinks it's great, dances along with her, imitating her to encourage her, make it more fun for her, the camera wobbling away. As part of her dance, she falls over backwards. She hangs over the cushions with her head dangling in the gap between her throne and the armrest and she can't get back up, she giggles. He helps her up, but not all the way, she gets stuck three-quarters of the way up, protesting and laughing at the same time.

When she's back on her throne, watching T.V., he asks: What's this? She studies him carefully, recognises something and, with a smile, brings her index finger to the tip of her nose. Clearly, with visible effort, she says: Nose.

To help her pronounce it, she makes the word longer, ending on a slightly slurred s. You can see that she's picturing the speech therapist, Gaby, who, focusing her attention on her mouth, the open lips pushed forward for emphasis, is demonstrating how to do it.

At the children's rehabilitation centre, they're surprised by her progress. It's not unusual for the speech centre to move to the right half of the brain, where it usually takes the place of spatial awareness, which the girl needs less urgently now – what's amazed them is the speed of her progress. She works hard, she's determined, stubborn. Every weekday Tereza takes her to the hospital, every time she has four or five hours of therapy. Then she has to rest.

The rapid results keep Renée motivated. Tereza and Steegman celebrate every step forward. But neither of them can prevent the fear that's growing along with the joy. The better it all goes, the better the prospects, the more scared they are of losing everything all at once.

She's walking. In the next clip she heads out of the kitchen, to the sunroom, and then into the garden. I freeze the picture and look at the light coming in, the intensity of the sun, the piece of garden, Tereza's clothes, as she reads a magazine in the corner of the sunroom, her shoes: possibly early autumn, warm behind the glass. October – Renée is walking. In the kitchen Steegman gives her a doughnut with pink icing, she holds it up to the camera like a trophy and then walks away. Heavy, laborious steps. She holds her knee rigid, her upper body hinges around the top of her thigh bone. Her lower leg sticks out at an awkward angle.

He protests, it's too soon. She's not allowed to do anything more than stand on her leg, Paul stressed that to them very clearly. Allowing her to walk by herself at this early stage is only going to teach her bad habits, the wrong way to walk, which will then be difficult to correct. Now she's looking for the path of least resistance, the easiest way to move forward. It's not just bad habits, she could also injure her muscles and tendons. Sprains, inflammation. In therapy she's only allowed to stand when she's wearing her brace. The other leg also has a brace to prevent overcompensation. The hard plastic has been specially made to fit and holds the calf, heel and sole of the foot at an angle of ninety degrees. At night she wears a different brace, just on her right leg, to stretch her calf muscle, which would otherwise shorten and increase the spasticity in her foot.

He sets off in pursuit. On his way outside he asks Tereza why she's not doing anything. She should have stopped Renée, she knows what Paul said. Why does he have to be the one who tells her off, the bad guy? Sometimes he'd like to be the one who says: Oh, go on. Let her. Just this once.

He walks after her, calmly, doesn't run, doesn't want her to panic, afraid she'll stumble over her own toes, which she can't lift. She seems to be following the path to the gate between the conifers, as usual. She's still wearing clothes from before, she's thick around the waist, a fold between hip and torso – she's about to explode. The effort of walking, the concentration it takes, makes her arm and hand cramp up in a spasm and rise to shoulder height by themselves. It's as if her brain wants to get the useless limb out of the way so it doesn't disturb her walking. The jerky movements make her lank hair swing from side to side.

Is this where it happens? Because of the memory this brings up of three, four months ago, when the walk to school was still so ordinary? When he didn't even realise it was paradise? Is this where he had the idea for the first chapter of T?

The gate has no lock, just a sliding bolt. The shed had been completely cleared out now, except for two sacks of potting soil and a rusty rake: a dark, damp place, it seemed five degrees colder than outside. I sat down against the birch tree in the corner of the garden. I kept still, as if I might be able to catch him, Renée darting ahead, jumping from slab to slab, towards the conifers. The exciting yet disappointing feeling that I'd never get any closer to Steegman than this. I stayed until it got dark, until the first bat arrived.

In her bedroom, at night, the red glow of the toadstool lamp, the little stars on the wall. Renée lies with both of her arms on top of the cover, as she was tucked in and instantly fell asleep. I turn up the volume and in the headphones I can hear both her breathing, slow, deep, and his, whistling through the nose hairs. No other sounds, or too quiet to be picked up by the microphone. Her right arm's trussed up in an instrument of torture: a mechanism with adjustable screws at her wrist that stretches her hand and bends back her fingers. Her teddy, "Bear" in the book, lies between her arms, with his head sticking up above the quilt.

212

He and Tereza take it in turns. It's certainly no chore. Ideally he'd always sleep beside his daughter. Ideally he'd like always to be so close to her, so peaceful. What could be more beautiful than his sleeping child, doing nothing but breathing, free until the morning from her concerns and limitations? He knows that they as parents create the illusion of security, the cosy, pink bedroom, Daddy or Mummy close by all night long. Even so, there's nowhere he himself feels safer than here, protected from life, from fate, making himself small instead of trying to act big, a child again beside his child. In armour made of fresh sheets, invisible beneath the mosquito net.

Bear keeps watch. He records him in close-up. It's just about possible to make out his eyes in the faint light. They look real. An expression as if he knows he's being filmed, slightly superior: you can film as long as you like, I won't even twitch, I can keep this up for days. A secret agent, a special envoy. At night he reports back about Renée to a higher authority. It's a bulky file by now. A hanging file.

Expectations for her arm are low. In fact, other than regaining control over her shoulder, there are none. Walking is relatively simple for healthy people: as soon as the thigh begins the movement, it's automatically completed by the lower leg swinging from the knee. The stepping movement is identical left and right, the legs always working together: an automatism. Arms exist independently of each other, the control system is specific. The fine motor skills of the hand are also extremely complex.

In the case of a brain injury, distorted signals give

conflicting instructions to one and the same muscle. Moving to the left *and* to the right, up *and* down, results in a standstill, an uncontrollable spasm.

She becomes deeply miserable when her hand refuses to work. She sits at the table, manipulating the hand as if it were a disobedient puppy, something that exists outside of herself. Why is Hand being so difficult? She's obviously too young to talk to about cerebral infarctions and the inevitable after-effects, it's too soon, too complicated. But her misery exposes them. It points an accusatory finger at them. They're lying by keeping the truth from her. Her sadness infects them, and continues to nag away at them even when Renée is feeling brave again, soon afterwards, and cheerful, and still in the dark.

Then there are three clips that stop abruptly. Renée doesn't want to be filmed. She hurries out of the room as soon as he approaches with his camera. She crawls under the table, behind the curtains. Her "no" is not open to interpretation: go away and take that thing with you! When he briefly pursues her, she starts screaming. She cries.

She must have seen herself on video.

He stops. He doesn't touch the camcorder again. He can't hurt her, that's unforgivable. The days come and go: getting up, washing, medication, rehabilitation, rest; the weeks, the months. And one morning he decides that he could give it another go – no, he *has to* – it's too good not to record. He wants to preserve as much as possible. He has a bird in the hand.

The traces in her hair have disappeared, the bald strip has grown out and been trimmed. She's lost some weight, her eyes are no longer encapsulated by the swelling and pinched into that fixed expression that marks out all unhealthily obese people as if they were genetically related. Spring is in the air. The buds of the furze beside the yew hedge burst open a few days ago. Lodewijk Wesselmans already has his lawn licked into shape. Renée is wearing trainers, a larger size, her braces hidden inside her trouser legs, her lower legs and feet as stiff as prostheses. Even so, she's busy, happily going round and round the living room. She's acting silly, speaking a made-up language. She bows, her circuits become smaller, now and then her foot slips out from under her, but she doesn't fall. His heart skips a beat every time. Everything she is doing she has had to learn. She is now imitating everything that came so naturally before, as well as she can manage with the other half of her brain after endless practice.

Ni hao. She keeps repeating it: *Ni hao*, singing, she learned it from Tereza, who's waiting in the doorway with Renée's coat. She asks what's keeping her little Chinese girl. Renée strikes a pose for the camera, legs open, one hand on her waist, she shakes her hips. Then she brings her face to the lens: *Ni hao.* It sounds like a question.

He admires her. Without a shadow of a doubt, she's the best mother Renée could have. Her warmth, her unfailing intuition. He thinks back to that evening, when it all began, in the company of friends – friends he should perhaps visit, research for his novel, he decides, with the camera still in his hand. Tereza had just returned from two months in China. She'd crossed the country by train. He was dreading having to listen to the rapturous account of yet another distant "backpacking" adventure. Everyone wanted to go trekking back then, had a list of countries you needed to see before you could get on with the rest of your life. The Far East, South America. Yemen. He dreamed of an open-top sports car and Monte Carlo. He preferred to do his dreaming at home. Tereza was his polar opposite, wasn't scared to dress in young unknown designers who would never become famous. Creations she wore as if they were off the peg, outfits other people would be pointed at for wearing – other people, not her. He laughed until he cried: the Chinese were rude and smelly, shamelessly hawking up phlegm, spitting in the train, forcing her to buy expensive passes for God knows what, driving her and other backpackers out of the hotel in the middle of the night like livestock, onto a bus, then high up a mountain, which remained shrouded in mist, refusing to reveal the most spectacular sunrise in the world, then being chased back to the bus practically with a stick: back to bus, back to bus! She told the story with infectious glee, about her own hopelessness, about her failure.

She's not here; visiting a friend, or a day in town, or stretched out in a hot bath with Kundera, her favourite author. It's about six o'clock. Renée's hungry, she's at the table, sitting on the side by the windows. At the same height as her head, the branches sticking out from the yew hedge catch the raking light that falls onto the path. He's put the soup on the heat, buttered slices of bread. A piano sonata, light, tinkling: Mozart. It's been a good day. Perhaps he's written some more of *T*, the book is growing inside his head, taking shape, and the fact that he's back at work is calming him. He loves being absent in each other's presence. When she comes and leans against him, bored, and plays with a button of his shirt, or studies his glasses from close up, asking unimportant questions and only half listening to the late, mumbled response. He loves watching as she eats, her inward focus.

She scoops the croutons out of the glass jar, into her mug, counts out eleven of them. The table is laid with a blue cloth, a rattan placemat. Just the fist of her right arm is on the table. Plate, mug, cutlery, everything nicely in the right place. Order. Neatness. She stirs the teaspoon in her mug, pops it into her mouth so that she can put it back down, clean, beside her plate, but the spoon, the soup, is hotter than anticipated: she screws her eyes shut, turns her head away with a jerk, hunches her shoulders protectively. Her right arm shoots up. She tries to catch his eye, to see his reaction, but there is none. So she too carries on as if nothing has happened. She smacks her lips a bit. To no-one in particular she says: This is very tasty. Theatrically, she opens her eyes wide as she says her elongated "veeery." The handle of the mug is facing into the room. She holds on to its rim as she turns the handle towards her, lets go, audibly sucks in air between her teeth, flaps her hand; she casts a quick glance at her father. The second time, she perseveres. She bends over the mug and blows so hard that her fringe flies up. Not so hard, he whispers. She blows more gently, slurps the soup, think it's still a little too hot. With the teaspoon, she lifts just a crouton up to her mouth. Then, the spoon drops into the mug and she leans back with her hands up, as in a silent movie – Mozart on the piano – eyes wide open, looking ahead, shocked at the heat on her tongue, which then turns out not to be so bad after all, she nods slowly, approvingly, puts her hand high up on her chest like a little old lady, and carries on tasting with primly pursed lips. As she takes some cheese from the edge of her plate, she realises he is silently laughing. And suddenly serious, now a girl of four and no longer a comic actress, she asks: Are you laughing? The camera begins to shake. Are you laughing at me?

She goes on eating the chunks of cheese. He asks her to put her arm on the table. It's important for her shoulder, so that it doesn't end up drooping. He asks her again: Put your arm up on the table nicely. She calmly finishes what's in her mouth and says: I will if you ask nicely. Would you please put your arm on the table? She says: Dear Renée. Sweet Renée. She holds her head at an angle: Please? Please. She's enjoying the cheese, says: Cheeeese, cheese . . . Say it: Cheeeese. She holds a chunk up to her eye. He says: Now please put your arm on the table. She says, in a squeaky little voice: Please? Again the camera shakes, I laugh along with him. Playfully, she holds up an admonishing finger: Please? Please. She finishes the cheese, without putting her arm on the table. Veeery tasty.

Outside, at the bottom of the garden, Renée is standing almost in the cherry laurel. She's holding her arms nicely next to her body, her feet together; she's beaming. Hello, my name's Renée and I'm a faaabulous singer. With a gaze that sees nothing and no-one, she improvises a fast, challenging dance, while singing the same line over and over, something by one of her favourite girl bands. In the background, there's laughter, clapping. She quickly gets out of breath, but it's too soon to give up; in a completely different key, with the same passion and persistence, she goes on to repeat a different line. She has bunches above her ears, feels them moving on her head, gives them an extra shake.

She interrupts the performance to ask him to stop filming for a moment. She's hot, takes off her woollen waistcoat with the Mexican design. Ready, Daddy? Arms beside her body, feet together.

After a few minutes, she's just panting the same two words. She laughs at herself. She's about to drop down onto the grass when she thinks of something else. A song about Little Red Riding Hood from a children's T.V. show. To the beat of the song, she takes big steps, walks around in a circle, wagging her finger. Tereza helps her out with the second line, about taking biscuits to Grandmother in the forest.

He includes Grandma, his mother, in the shot. The trees are chilly and bare, except for the old magnolia, beneath which Grandma's watching the show with a teary smile. The crown of the tree is four times higher than its leaning, twisting trunk: hundreds, thousands of pink-white flowers, glowing in the sun. As stunning as a panorama.

His father is kneeling nearby in green overalls and a lumberjack shirt, surrounded by the posts and planks of a self-assembly kit. A new swing, there's a red plastic seat among the wood. Four holes have been dug in the lawn to anchor the swing in quick-setting concrete. He looks up and shouts over to him, teasing: Hey, this is where the action is! Then he goes back to studying the instructions.

They don't grow closer until around his thirtieth.

Father and son. Both parents, both willing to be under-standing. They still don't see each other very often, the difference isn't spectacular. It's hard for him to pinpoint the change. One day some odd jobs needed doing on someone's house. One morning they were there, passing tools to each other. It didn't seem out of the ordinary, it felt as if it had never been any different. When the ward-robe was screwed together, the firewood split, the fitting mounted, the front door painted, the gutter repaired, the swing anchored, his father asked how it was going with his book, and he said: fine.

They prove to be an excellent team, they back each other up, they're on the same side. They drink beer when they're thirsty. With pride, self-mockery, he displays the blisters on his writer's hands. His father volunteers that his back is where he's feeling it, he's not getting any younger. But his father's fitter than he is, tougher, hardened from working in a factory since the age of four-teen. He carries his wisdom in his hands, beneath thick layers of calloused skin – working together teaches him how his father thinks. He's glad to serve him, he feels humble and content with his background, which for a long time he resisted with his literature. He is relieved. Their years in Zingene, under the same roof but on differ-ent planets, are over for good. Nothing else needs to be said or explained. They sweat and they hit nails on the head.

His parents, the parents of Andy Boogaart and Petra van Rie *and* Sandra Volckaert were all still living in a radius of less than a hundred metres in the same part of Zingene when news of Sandra's mysterious death and the rumours about an arrest warrant for Steegman sent shockwaves throughout the country, which soon reached France, England, Germany and Israel, where translations of *T* had been published simultaneously. Local authority housing from the mid-1970s. Most of the original residents had outgrown their surroundings; they hadn't packed their bags but in every way they could, up to and including the facade of the house, they'd adapted their homes to suit their modern requirements and new status. His parents were said to have turned down an offer from their son six months earlier, shortly before the publication of the book. Steegman had moved house, though, a self-imposed exile, presumably to France. The Alsace countryside. The Cévennes. The Midi-Pyrénées. Or Ireland, tweets that he'd been seen near Michel Houellebecq's house, with whom Steegman shares several publishers. Blurred photographs from Hungary; Tereza is a distant descendant of illustrious Slavic nobility. I thought it more likely that they'd have wanted to keep as little distance as possible between Renée and her grandparents. Even Alsace is a long drive.

During those few days when the arrest warrant was brewing, I read the final chapter of *T* several times. I won't have been the only one. It's the finest chapter of the book, a small epistolary novel in its own right. T has finally retreated behind the fence of his country estate and enters into an intense correspondence with Sandra V.: a highly charged sparring match between two razor-sharp minds. Within the space of fifty pages, Steegman had managed to tilt at the crown of *Les Liaisons dangereuses*. Breathtaking. This tour de force made an impact on the perception of the book as a whole.

On the final page, Sandra V. is found dead in her apartment. On the table is a handwritten letter, saying goodbye in words that cannot be misunderstood. A prostitute, forty-two years old. Suicide. But the reader intuitively senses that there's more going on. That the farewell letter could just as easily have been addressed to T. A letter he could have coaxed out of her only after a correspondence such as theirs. With premeditation. With murder on his mind.

A frequent compliment regarding the book was that after reading the final word you went straight back to the beginning and started reading again; you have no choice, you can't rest, you feel that you've missed something, that you've read something incorrectly in a novel that is actually crystal clear. That the truth is there for the taking. Another compliment was about the voice of Sandra V.: it was almost impossible to believe Steegman had written the letters of both T and Sandra. It was as if the letters had been plucked from a genuine correspondence, so realistic, so authentic.

The police found only one letter in Sandra Volckaert's flat: on the table, beside a very well-thumbed paperback. A copy of the farewell letter in T. Sandra Volckaert had died in the same way as the character in the novel who was apparently based on her. She'd written the letter by hand. The investigation ultimately turned up no significant leads. At a chaotic press conference, which was broadcast live, the examining magistrate declared that the victim had died by suicide and that the author named Emiel Steegman was therefore – he stared accusingly into the explosion of flashlights – not under suspicion.

But the whirlwind raged on. The hunger of both media and public was insatiable. It was impossible to keep up with the rumours; some would never die down. People linked and shared and commented all over Facebook. Twitter was a cacophony. Columnists became fishwives, attacking one another. People who had only recently discovered the existence of Sandra Volckaert: everyone had an opinion about her death.

Sandra had been murdered by shady characters in her own family, conveniently making use of the successful novel so that suspicion would fall on Steegman. They were drug dealers. Exported stolen cars to Poland and Bulgaria. They manufactured ecstasy tablets. They were involved in human trafficking from Africa. Had ties to the Chinese gambling mafia. Steegman had committed the perfect murder, more cunningly than T in the novel. After all, no-one would believe he'd be so foolish as to do away with Sandra Volckaert in such an ostentatious manner. A masterful plan that involved writing a novel, waiting for the story to become known to a wide audience. Hollywood would film it, screenwriters were already at work. Wouldn't it be a great irony if John Malkovich were to play Steegman – Vicomte de Valmont in *Dangerous Liaisons*? Sandra was a manipulative bitch, even worse than in the book, she'd laid down her life just to get the last word, her ultimate revenge. She couldn't stand it that she didn't possess a jot of talent herself, and so she chose to sully the name of a great author with her cowardly deed. Steegman was a gutless jerk who needed to be smoked out of his hole in the forests or mountains and then pilloried in the Glass Street and stoned by the whores. Entirely without scruples, playing free and easy with the life of a defenceless, single woman for his own personal gain. An overblown upstart. He wasn't even worth talking about.

A book of condolences was created for Sandra Volckaert. Groups supporting Steegman sprang up all over Facebook. The slanging matches on internet forums intensified, and for a while *T* disappeared from the bookshelves as vandals tore the last page from the book whenever they could. The local policeman, a fan of Steegman, who'd found Sandra and who'd let his mouth run away with him that same evening to a journalist from a local radio station – the spark in the powder keg – received death threats in the form of handwritten copies of *that* letter, or at least it was made clear to him that he'd be better off committing suicide while he still had the chance.

Pieters was in his element. On just one evening, I saw the previously unknown criminal lawyer on three talk shows. He'd already won, his performances were like a triumphal march through prime-time television. His fortune was made, it was written all over his sallow proletarian features. A wispy little moustache that curled inward and was a completely different colour from the hair on his head, which stuck up in wet spikes on top, with the rest left dry and unkempt. Murder and manslaughter weren't options, he didn't even stand a chance of making a case for involuntary assault and wounding. Libel and defamation, on the other hand . . . But one way or another: a trial. That must have been his thinking. Just as long as there was a trial, as long as he could get Steegman in front of a judge. With the current commotion and attention, it would be as if the writer were appearing before the Assize

Court. No matter what the sentence, a "guilty" would make him guilty of murder.

After the first day of the trial, the mayor of Zingene decided to establish a press-free zone in part of the housing estate. The British newspaper photographers scoffed in disbelief. The houses of the Steegmans and the Volckaerts received 24-hour police protection. TV crews moved into the village, even the national evening news programme resorted to inane street interviews. I was furious. Not sensationalism, not like the others, but a report about the impact of this media scrum on a small community. A baker. An elderly woman. The local priest. Insanity that they, by producing such reports, afraid of the competition, were only exacerbating.

The lark scene – the impetus of the plot; I could follow the judge's reasoning. But I also understood the ensuing commotion, caused, after all, by the man who had previously urged both parties to be reasonable, as he warned those in court to remain calm or risk being charged with contempt after the defence had described the final section of the novel as nothing but fiction and argued that there had never been any contact between Steegman and the late lamented Sandra Volckaert, and Pieters smiling, slowly shaking his head, supported by all the tumult, as he rose imperiously from his seat.

This development surprised everyone. A judge who sought clarification in a novel, being of the opinion that nothing could be said about the impact of the all-important final section if he did not know the "essential truth" of the lark scene, the seed of the intrigue, the origin of the epistolary battle that, years later, would result in a fight to the death. He wanted some insight into the degree of fictionalisation at this key moment, before passing judgement on the impact of the consequences, even if they were a fabrication. He suspended the session indefinitely.

"The Trial of the Novel", read the headline in the *Guardian* the next morning, an allusion to Kafka. The newspaper editorials were unanimous: this could be the death knell for literature. Who, after the Steegman trial, would slave away to produce penetrating prose, or dare to publish it, whether based on their own experiences or not, if it might lead readers to engage in a process of identification? Fiction so realistic that it apparently became dangerous, or – in the words of Pieters the lawyer – might offend the honour of the reader, in this case Sandra Volckaert.

In the lead-up to the testimonies of Andy Boogaart and Petra van Rie, Sky News found Farmer Tuyt, in a retirement home in Wevelgele, five minutes' drive from Zingene. They'd planted him in his armchair, in the corner of the room, under a crucifix with a dried-up palm stuck behind it. The buttoned-up collar of his shirt hung loosely around his neck, a pale old man with red-veined cheeks from working outdoors. He knew Emiel Steegman. Yep. Did he know he'd been included in a world-famous book? Yep. His daughter acted as interpreter, when he said "yep," she nodded. He knew. A woman who had never been able to overcome the effects of the full-fat cow's milk, the butter and the lard of her childhood. They showed him images, recorded earlier that day, of the street, now old and dusty, at one time his land, where once, on a particular day, when everything suddenly went quiet, a lark rose up out of the long grass. Farmer Tuyt looked at the microphone that was hovering high up in his room, out of shot. Yep. His daughter nodded. He knew it had happened there.

Neither Andy Boogaart nor Petra van Rie seemed the type to commit perjury, or even to dare to consider it. Conscientious – Petra had her own shop, with her husband, fruit and vegetables, Andy had been a foreman at a large horticultural company for years – and was obviously intimidated by the events and by the court. Because their statements were so different from the realistic and vivid scene in T, and from each other, they caused furrowed brows in both camps. The judge must have determined that their memories had been polished by time, rearranged, touched up until they were acceptable, but still perfectly in line with the personalities that Steegman had assigned to them in the relevant scenes from their childhood. Andy insisted that Steegman hadn't made him do anything at all. He had never, ever, been anyone's running boy. Petra said the lark scene had never happened. That Steegman and she had been boyfriend and girlfriend and always went around together. He thought Sandra was stuck-up. Sorry she had to say it, but he didn't think Sandra was very pretty.

Le Monde described Steegman's sentence – moral damages of 1 euro – as a bargain, like a Prix Goncourt with the winner not receiving but paying a symbolic pittance, awarded to what was perhaps the last important literary novel.

They were right about the first point: T conquered the

227

United States and was number one in Japan for twenty-seven weeks. But not about the second. Eight years on, it's quite clear that the trial actually revitalised literature. The huge amount of attention has produced a new generation of writers, headstrong, unconventional, and convinced of the impact of the novel.

Had there really been no contact between Steegman and Sandra Volckaert? The writer didn't attend the trial. So that he would not have to answer that question under oath? Had he tracked down the woman when he was writing *T*? Had a relationship with her? Written letters that were subsequently destroyed? Or was his blind, literary fabrication of her adult emotions simply a bull's-eye? If not, then this woman, who was not after all a prostitute but a humble post office employee who worked nights in the sorting office, would have felt nothing when she read the book, would have shrugged her shoulders, maybe, just maybe, have taken legal action, but she'd never have taken her own life like that.

Was Sandra Volckaert jealous of Sandra V., of her life, a life she'd like to have led? Did she feel as if those letters, via the novel, were addressed to her? A continuation of what they'd both found in the long grass? He, fathomed for the first and last time, or rather, unmasked; she, giving him the impression that she'd discovered some pleasure in her assault, perhaps even desire in her "revelation". Then, almost thirty years later, he imagines in his book a life for her in which she has become public property. She finds happiness in freeing herself. She no longer has to be anyone, an untold burden falls from her shoulders. Over and over again, she becomes the woman the customer projects onto her. She has ceased to exist, but at the same time she is living a thousand lives.

Was that what Sandra Volckaert had in mind?

He does it secretly. He makes sure Renée doesn't notice. Just a small gap between the net curtain and the bay window. They've already said goodbye at the front door, a kiss, an encouraging pat on the bum, no drama: see you later. It is the child psychologist who is stage-managing this new development, seven or eight months after the stroke. Renée needs some independence. It's better if Tereza stops taking her to the centre. Although she still has years of intensive rehabilitation to go, she's made great progress; the wheelchair was returned months ago. They just need to have the courage to leave her to her own devices, to entrust others with her care. They have to learn to let go.

Tereza stands behind him, peeping through the crack. There's a taxi service that operates throughout the whole country. The driver – today a young man with a white-blond beard, friendly smile, modern clothes but smart, a bright expression – helps Renée through the sliding door and into the minibus. Neither of them wants to let go. That's their child, there on the pavement, in jeans and a pink jacket, with a little rucksack packed with fruit juice, mineral water, two slices of bread with cheese spread, a chocolate waffle. Paper tissues.

Even when he leaves her on her own in a room at home, panic sometimes takes hold of him. Uncontrollable visions. He comes back from the kitchen with a glass of milk and Renée's lying motionless on the rug. He empties the letterbox, goes to the toilet, writes. He wasn't there. Over the head of every child, every parent, hangs a sword of Damocles. The one above Renée's head glitters and sparkles and gleams in the sunlight, in the pouring rain, in the dead of night.

They look through the gap, perhaps they're seeing her for the last time. As the bus drives out of the street, they disappear into different rooms, or they hug awkwardly in a part of the house where it feels strange. The last time: they'll be battling that thought for another five hours or so. Until the white minibus pulls up outside. They stand in the hallway. They wait to open the door until the driver and Renée are halfway down the path. They hear her voice through the frosted glass.

She is dancing in the sunroom. A prelude by Chopin, an impromptu by Schubert makes her move gently. She integrates her disability into her delicate ballet; owning her flaws, she no longer thinks about it, she hears music and transforms it into dance. She doesn't appear to be bothered by Steegman or his camera. It's just after noon. They've had a simple lunch: sausages, apple sauce, fried potatoes; Tereza's loading the dishwasher. This peaceful moment as a household gradually falls silent, ending in naps. Later, in stocking feet, the scent of coffee, the perfume of orange.

He wonders if there will come a day when the new, dancing Renée will make them forget the first Renée, instead of reminding them so sharply of her. How far off is that day, if it exists? He asks himself the question, in the sunroom. He thinks: isn't it easier for parents whose child is born disabled? Or not? Is it the other way around? Should he fear the day when the new Renée has completely supplanted the old one? Or won't he have to choose between them? Will the girls eventually merge together, as if one of them never ceased to exist, and the other has never been any different? Holding them up to the light and sliding them over each other without seeing any difference.

Tereza is filming. For the first time, tonight I see Steegman in shot. He's driving the car, she's sitting next to him. A line of trees flashes past behind him. He protests. He's wearing his hair longer, blonder, than I picture when I think of him. He tells Tereza to stop now; Renée, in the back, encourages her mum, who laughs, conspiratorially: what goes around comes around. He makes a grab for the camcorder and the clip stops: he is looking angrily above the lens.

There's no sign of it in his face as yet. A little pale, it's morning, he didn't sleep too well. Perhaps he took Naramig two, three hours ago, and the naratriptan, by constricting the blood vessels, is preventing the onset of a migraine. What I see is the laughter lines around his eyes, which, as he's got older, have grown too deep to disappear when the laughter stops. His eyes are not swollen, the cheekbone beneath the frame of the glasses is still intact – not an ugly man, a dimple in his chin. It's too soon to see anything; in this image the tumour behind his left eye must be the size of a sesame seed, a grain of rice, a coffee bean. Behind the eyeball, out of sight. He doesn't know about it yet. An itch, the occasional migraine, that's about it. A gradual horror that in less than ten years will have devoured his entire face, except for his lower jaw. Bone, eyes, skin. The obituary makes a conspicuous allusion to a natural death. "Thankful for his life, right to the end."

A big speed bump jolts the car. Renée, who was staring out of the window, lost in thought, looks around, searches for something on the back seat, on the floor. Her head angled as if to see Tereza's lap, she asks anxiously where her bear is. Where's Bear? She was going to look after Bear, wasn't she? Hadn't she said so to Mummy when everything was ready on the table, that she wanted to take care of her bear herself? She wants Bear! She kicks the back of Tereza's seat. Steegman tells her to calm down; take a look in the bag. Tereza rummages around in a bag at her feet, finds the teddy straight away. Is it Bear? Sweetheart, you can see it's Bear, can't you? Renée leans far forward and yanks him out of her mother's hand. She lays him on his tummy, inspects something beside his round tail. Then she picks at a thread in the seam around his neck. She looks into both eyes, at length, seriously. Finally she hugs him to her chest. She sighs. It's Bear.

Look! A strong breeze is making the magnolia snow, the petals swirl down diagonally in a thick cloud, covering the lawn with a carpet of pink and white. They're in the bathroom on the first floor; the tap's dripping into a full bath, the fresh layer of foam is crackling. Look! He's pointing the camera at Renée beside him, undressed, she doesn't look to see if he's seeing what she's seeing. She points with a straight arm. He kneels to film her face, full of wonder. He zooms in, bringing the eye on his side, big and brown and gleaming, with long eyelashes, closer and closer. In her eye, silhouetted, the window, the tree, the fairy-tale snowstorm. I know what I felt when I heard them breathing at night in the pink glow of her bedroom. I am *so* close to Steegman. I *am* Steegman . . .

They're in the living room, ready to go. It's a big day. He asks her what day it is today. Where's Renée going? She's going to proper school. Back to proper school? For the first time? She nods. Just a couple of hours, for now. But . . . with her teacher, in the infants' class? At proper school? One corner of her mouth turns up. A nod. She says she's so proud that she's almost crying. He says she has every reason to be proud, but there's surely no reason to cry? She listens to what he says. Then she cries.

Soon the mood lightens again. Tereza and Renée walk ahead of him. Something is blossoming in the grass, clover perhaps, he doesn't know. The brown, shrivelled petals have been raked together under the magnolia. Renée tries to jump from one slab to the next, Tereza, in a mid-length beige trench coat with horn buttons, epaulettes and a wide collar, which is hanging loose but still fits nicely around her waist, says Renée had better walk instead. If she falls, she'll make her trousers green.

They have plenty of time to watch. They're walking beside each other now, about five metres behind their daughter. The path. The street. The school. The way the inside of her right heel hits the left foot with every step. First he says that she's being big and brave, then that she has to lift her knee nice and high. That's right! Tereza takes his hand; they can't say anything to each other.

Soon she'll go to school part-time, alongside her re-habilitation. The psychologist thinks that Renée, with a few minor adjustments, will be able to attend ordinary school classes. She'll need a little more time, and she'll get tired more quickly.

The headmistress has positioned herself in the centre of the empty entrance hall. She crouches down just in front of Renée, holds her by the shoulders and says she's so happy to see her again. She gives her head a little shake. So happy. Come on, she must be curious about her class-mates. After a brief pause, Renée accepts the outstretched hand.

The corridor is long and straight, the infant classes are located furthest from the entrance. On the left, classes at work; on the right, windows from around neck height to the ceiling. On the wall, components of a P.C., attached to wooden boards years ago. Keyboard. Mouse. Photographs of local wildlife. A long line of water-colours. On the window ledge, decapitated plastic bottles, filled with sand, with flowers of painted cardboard and aluminium foil growing in them. Steegman is desperately nervous. Their echoing steps. The proximity of the school playground.

Left at the end of the corridor, a little further and then right, to the swing doors. Beyond those, the infants' corri-dor. The teacher looks around the corner of the classroom. She claps her hands, then squats and opens her arms. Renée allows her to give her a hug and says: Hello, Miss. The coat hooks offer a diversion from the ensuing awk-wardness: she can choose one of the pictures that haven't been taken yet. She hesitates. Balloon. A balloon, that's a lovely picture, everyone agrees. The teacher stands by to help her take off her coat. The children are sitting in a semicircle in a cosy corner of the classroom. Quiet as mice. What do you say? Hello, Renée!

They agree on half an hour before the lunch break. They want to keep her out of the crowds this first time, it could frighten her, she's still very unsure.

It happens right in front of his eyes, on the way home. He hears it but there's no time to intervene. The tip of her sneaker tripping, in the middle of the street. It's not tiredness, one side of the road surface is slightly higher than the other, with old-fashioned concrete slabs. No traffic, or he'd have been holding her hand. It's not actual tripping, her shoe collides with the high lip. The sound is followed by an excruciating silence as both he and Renée know that she's heading helplessly for the ground. She disappears from view, it's too late. You never get used to it. Every fall is the first. Her toes swing forward just above the ground, in a shoe that's a size bigger because of the brace, so the slightest bump can make her stumble. This is more than stumbling. She smacks right into the concrete. A dead thud.

It's not the first time it's happened right in front of his eyes. It makes him sick with anger. He feels a murderous hatred: she's so vulnerable and so severely tested. Always on her hand, which jerks up as she falls, always in the same place, on and below the knuckles of her little finger and her ring finger, a thick, cracked scab, an ugly wound that never has the chance to heal.

He's with his daughter before she starts screaming.

He picks her up, quickly, easily, snatches her away from the ground as if she were lying in a fire, almost roughly. He is a single clenched muscle, he doesn't say a word. She must feel the silent strength of her father, stronger than the injustice that struck her down.

He carries her home, she cries into his neck. Their embrace could not be tighter, she becomes part of him, weightless. He could carry on walking all day, if their house were that far from the school. He wouldn't mind. His nose in her hair.

2

Willem is standing up in his bed, head above the bars. Blinking, he laughs towards my voice in the light. He's slept for a long time, it's almost eight o'clock. I pick him up in his sleeping bag. His one cheek is glowing, the other feels colder than the room.

"Have you been up all night?" Valeria looks at my clothes. She's noticed my side of the bed hasn't been slept in. I sit down on the edge and let Willem crawl towards her. She says, "Come here, my little angel."

Up here on the eighth floor, the bedroom has a panoramic view of the snowy roofs in the inner city. The early light turns the hazy vapour trails pink and the more distant ones dark purple. Medieval plumes of smoke billow from chimneys.

"How was it?"

While I search for the right word, something more precise than "good" or "interesting", she asks if I've found anything, something about Sandra Volckaert.

"No," I say. "No indications that they saw each other, or had any contact. No."

"Well, what, then?" Holding Willem to her chest, she moves to the edge of the bed, stands up and disappears into the bathroom to change his nappy.

"Actually it's just Renée. The way the girl fought after her stroke. Her heroism."

"But did you find out anything about Steegman?"

"Yes. I think so . . ."

"And is it any good? Can you use it in that book of yours?"

I hear a touch of resentment in her voice. That book of yours. I've been up all night, I'd like to sleep soon. Why am I being so reticent about a book that's due to be published soon in large numbers? A book I'll have to talk to strangers about for months? She's jealous. Steegman was already there. He was there before she came.

As if she's talking to Willem on the changing table, she says, "I don't understand why he didn't pick a different name for Sandra. It would have saved him and so many other people a whole lot of trouble."

I sit down on her side of the bed, leaf through the book on her bedside table. The award-winning French debut novelist has dark eyes and a neatly trimmed beard. I'm close to the large window, on the other side of which the atmosphere is now splitting the light into flaming colours, once again obscuring the view of the icy light years between the stars.

"It's a red herring," I say. "Her name, Sandra V. And it would only work if her name in the book was almost the same. Sandra V. is T's secret, Sandra Volckaert isn't Steegman's. Not really."

Last night's full nappy falling to the floor. The adhesive strip of a new one. "Come again?"

I put the book down, open at the right page, spine

facing up. "I don't think Steegman is – *was* – as crazy or obsessive as T. He amplified a part of himself. Do you get it?"

"Yes, I get it, thank you very much. What do you mean by a red herring?"

"I'm not saying it's not bad. Of course it's sexual assault, certainly by today's standards. I'm not trying to justify it: it was wrong. But it also seems to me like a game, admittedly a game that got out of hand, but one that any pubescent teenager could have played. You don't think so? Look, if you describe it the way Steegman did in *T* it seems like a big deal, but maybe another writer would have turned it into something more playful. Could have."

"You reckon?"

"It's not like I approve. You won't hear me saying it doesn't matter . . . I'm just saying I think he used it as a red herring. And the misdirection would only work if it was presented as realistically as possible. With a name alluding to the woman in question."

"Do you know what I think? I think he described it pretty damn well." She appears in the doorway with Willem in her arms. Cellulite where his bare legs are pressed together under his own weight. "But we were talking about secrets . . ."

Willem says "Daddy" twice and drops forward. His little feet slap against the floor. He holds out his arms to me. "Pick up."

"There is no secret . . . At least I don't think there's a secret. And no matter how strange, how paradoxical, it might sound, that could be the reason he went into hiding. He was no more than his books. I think he thought his life was banal . . . And he was afraid that banality would devalue his work."

We have breakfast. We divide up the newspaper, we read and eat without saying anything. When we've been sitting in silence for a while, I say, "That explains the films . . ."

She turns her head to look at me.

"I had an email from Felix, by the way. They're genuine, the cassettes. They're the originals, I mean. If he had copies, he wouldn't have sent the originals. All the clips are about Renée. No editing, raw footage."

"Maybe he's got digital copies."

"So why send the cassettes?"

"He was serious about it. That at least is certain." She starts clearing the table. "He wanted the package to make an impression. He wanted to saddle you with the responsibility. One last attempt, from his sickbed, to take control of the situation. Because he clearly wants his daughter to have a prominent role in your book." She picks up the tray and walks to the kitchen.

Through the two cracks in the doors, I catch a glimpse of my office on the other side of the hallway, part of the bookshelf, which is filled with all the Ts that have been published, nearly all the reprints worldwide. All the graphic novel versions, movie versions, editions in Braille. All the Murderers. Twenty metres of Steegman.

"Her name is Renée," I say.

"What?"

Her question comes a moment too late. She heard me, understood what I said.

"She's called Renée. His daughter."

240

"Do you think I don't know that?"

After five minutes of industrious tidying in the kitchen, she asks if I want another coffee. Drying her hands, she comes into the room and repeats her question.

"That explains the films," I say. "He thought his life was too banal to warrant a biography. He didn't think it was worth a book. Renée's life was, though. Her achievement was greater than his. I think that's what he's trying to tell me."

The tea towel hangs limp in her hands.

"You think the films are his attempt to put a stop to his biography? Is that what you mean?"

"Yes."

"Emiel Steegman? The famous writer of *T*? Isn't that, well, a really rather naive thought?"

"I consider the writer of *T* to be perfectly capable of doing exactly that. He's serious about this, the cassettes are original. It's not a trick. I think it's genuine."

A vast blanket of clouds as wide as the sky slides across the sun. Ten centimetres of snow are forecast. As darkness falls, Willem is illuminated by the T.V., a ghostly apparition. He's kneeling against the arm of the sofa and watching in fascination as a man dressed in green and red and yellow plays a song on his decorated guitar in the garden of a white wooden house, with dancing, laughing children all around him.

She perches on the chair opposite me. "Maybe, on his deathbed. But even so, even if his intention is as romantic as you imagine, even then, at death's door, he must have realised that if you abandoned the project, someone else would still write his biography."

I imagine his deathbed. He's at home, his bed is in the living room by the window overlooking the walled garden with the pond, like a park, which he can see only in his memory now, through a haze of morphine. The blue flashes of the diving kingfisher. He searches for the name, kingfisher, he's sure he knows it, he searches slowly, curious as a child to see if he will find it in time.

"No," I say. "He wasn't stupid."

She shakes her head. "No, he can't have been that stupid." She laughs a little.

As we approach the point where we can't sit there any longer without saying something, she wipes her hands on the tea towel again, and stands up. She asks if I'd like another coffee.

3

Late that evening I watch the news report again, in my office. It's very short. All of the news channels showed the same, brief item. Tereza must have made a deal. One camera crew is permitted to film a report of one minute. It's that or nothing. She doesn't need the money. Outside, the press remain at a respectful distance from the church. That was the second thing that struck me: a church.

During the service, I recognise family members. Friends. Colleagues. Publishers. The occasional dignitary.

I play the last eleven seconds in slow motion.

She walks beside her mother, who is hiding behind a fine mesh veil. She's wearing a beautiful, black coat with a pelerine cape and a double row of buttons, black tights and classic patent leather shoes. She turned fourteen in August. Her hair is short, an angled bob that follows the line of her jaw and ends in playful points.

I recognise her, I see the girl of almost five, even though, strictly speaking, that girl has entirely disappeared. This is a young woman. I freeze the image. The tawny skin. The warm brown of eye, lash and brow. The dimple low on her chin, a small indentation, no more than a gentle slope, subtly rounding off the contours of her face. Subtle.

This is a beauty that whispers, but will be heard by anyone who stops to listen.

She is not crying, she is very much present, aware of her surroundings. When I start the clip again, she walks on calmly, without limping or faltering, lifting both knees equally, arm in arm and in step with her mother.

It's her right hand, no doubt about it.

With a fluid movement, she brings the white flower over the matt wood, above his legs, to the spot where Tereza's flower lies. She holds the stem between thumb and forefinger; only her little finger appears to want to stretch out. Showing the very slightest hesitation, which seems to me more an indication of repressed grief, she separates the tips of her fingers, releases the flower and smoothly moves her arm back beside her body. The imitation so perfect that the difference can no longer be seen.

Leabharlanna Poiblí Chathair Bhaile Átha Cliath
Dublin City Public Libraries

PETER TERRIN represents a unique voice in contemporary literature, touching on universal and highly topical themes. He is considered by critics to be a literary maverick and a masterful stylist. He is also an avid collector of vintage typewriters. He won a European Literature Prize for *The Guard*, and the A.K.O. Literature Prize, the Dutch equivalent of the Man Booker Prize, for *Post Mortem*, in which a fictional writer wins a fictional counterpart prize, The Golden Belly Band.

LAURA WATKINSON is a translator from Dutch, Italian and German. She lives in a tall, thin house on a canal in Amsterdam. She has translated works by authors including Cees Nooteboom and Tonke Dragt.

Acknowledgements

Many thanks to everyone who contributed to this book in one way or another. In chapter 14 of Part One, Steegman must have taken inspiration from Hans den Hartog Jager's essay in *N.R.C. Handelsblad* on 2 May, 2008, about looking and being seen. I would like to thank the Flemish Literature Fund, the Dutch Foundation for Literature, and the Province of West Flanders for their support. My thanks to V. for her unconditional love.

Peter Terrin

THE GUARD

Translated from the Dutch by David Colmer

Harry and Michel live in the basement of a luxury apartment block, guarding its residents. Over the course of a weekend, the residents leave the block one by one – all apart from a man on floor 29. In the grey, airless monotony of the basement, Harry and Michel stick to their posts.

The world might be at war or plunged into nuclear winter; they may be the last inhabitants in the city. All they know is that if they are vigilant, "the organization" will reward them: promotion to an elite cadre of security officers remains their shining goal, and their days are punctuated by vivid dreams of everything they are missing.

But what if there were no-one left to guard? And if the promised third officer arrives, how would he fit into Michel and Harry's studied routine of boredom and paranoia?

MACLEHOSE PRESS

www.maclehosepress.com

Subscribe to our quarterly newsletter